PRAISE FOR PETER MAYLE'S *Caper* SERIES
*Featuring Sam Levitt*

"Wine and food aficionados will find much to savor. . . .
Light, funny and packed with a menu's worth of scrump-
tious descriptions of exceptional dinners and drinks."
—*USA Today*

"A succession of excellent repasts and leisurely ambles, which
Mayle depicts with painterly ease and signature *savoir vivre*.
. . . Pure Provence." —*National Geographic Traveler*

"A lighthearted romp through Bordeaux and Marseille, in
which picking the right restaurant, choosing the best dish
on the menu and, of course, finding the perfect wine . . . to
accompany the feast is every bit as important as catching
the thief." —*Los Angeles Times*

"Cinematic. . . . Meals are lovingly described, scenery comes
to life, paragraphs take long floral detours. And everyone
is blessed with hypersensitive taste buds. . . . By the time
Levitt returns to America, readers will have learned much
about the history of winemaking, the key wine regions,
various auction houses, critics and books—and even how
to lift fingerprints from bottles."
—*The New York Times Book Review*

"Mayle sends readers on a breezy excursion to southern France's least appreciated city in this entertaining crime novel filled with amiable digressions into the history, cuisine, and local culture of Marseille." —*Publishers Weekly*

"Provides a delightful behind-the-scenes tour of France and its wines, a satisfyingly satirical view of materialistic excesses in America, a mystery that keeps the reader guessing, and a pleasing, robust finish." —*The Philadelphia Inquirer*

"Abundant with luscious descriptions of the gastronomic delights of France. . . . Mayle's international caper is the vehicle for his exposition of all things French: countryside vineyards, brilliant seaside sunsets, chateau wine cellars, exquisitely prepared dishes, and, of course, wine."
—*The Free Lance-Star* (Fredericksburg)

"Relentlessly entertaining. . . . Mayle has concocted a shameless guilty–pleasure bonbon in *The Vintage Caper*."
—*The News-Observer* (Raleigh, NC)

"[Mayle] knows his wines and cuisines, evident in this mystery featuring gourmand-investigator Sam Levitt. Readers can vicariously enjoy world travel, great meals and memorable bottles of vino." —*The Sacramento Bee*

PETER MAYLE

# The Marseille Caper

Peter Mayle is the author of twelve previous books, six of them novels. A recipient of the Légion d'Honneur from the French government for his cultural contributions, he has been living in Provence with his wife, Jennie, for twenty years.

Peter Mayle's *Encore Provence*, *French Lessons*, *A Good Year*, *Provence A–Z*, *Toujours Provence*, *The Vintage Caper*, and *A Year in Provence* are available in Vintage paperback.

# The Marseille Caper

# The Marseille Caper

## PETER MAYLE

VINTAGE BOOKS
A Division of Random House, Inc.
New York

The Library of Congress has cataloged the Knopf edition as follows:
Mayle, Peter.
The Marseille caper / Peter Mayle.—1st ed.
p. cm.
1. Real property—Fiction. 2. Marseille (France)—Fiction. I. Title.
PR6063.A8875M37 2012
823'.914—dc23   2012021744

Vintage ISBN: 978-0-307-74095-3

www.vintagebooks.com

*In memory of Allen Chevalier,*
*a good friend who made lovely wine*

*The Marseille Caper*

# One

Shock has a chilling effect, particularly when it takes the form of an unexpected meeting with a man from whom you have recently stolen three million dollars' worth of wine. Sam Levitt shivered and pulled his terrycloth robe closer around his body, still damp from an early-morning dip in the Chateau Marmont pool.

"Here." The man on the other side of the table—smiling, tanned, immaculate—slid a cup of coffee across to Sam. "Drink this. It will warm you up. Then we can talk." He leaned back and watched as that first infinitely welcome cup went down, then another, while Sam tried to gather his wits.

Sam was sitting with Francis "Sissou" Reboul. The last time they had met had been in Marseille, over a glass of champagne at Le Pharo, Reboul's clifftop palace with a billionaire's view of the Mediterranean. Sam, on assignment from an international insurance company, was hunting for several hundred bottles of vintage Bordeaux that had been stolen from the Hollywood home of Danny Roth, an entertainment lawyer with a weakness for fine wines. After a search that had taken him from L.A. to Paris to Bordeaux to Marseille, Sam had discovered the stolen bottles in Reboul's vast cellar. And, being a man who preferred direct action to long and tiresome negotiations with the authorities, he had stolen them back. That, he had thought, was that. A nice, neat job, with no complaints likely from the victim. But here was the victim himself, in the garden of the Chateau Marmont in Los Angeles, behaving for all the world like an acquaintance who was trying to be a friend.

"Perhaps I should have given you some warning," said Reboul, with a shrug, "but I only flew into Los Angeles last night—there's some business I need to attend to here—and I thought I would take the opportunity to come and say *bonjour*." He took a card from his top pocket and pushed it across the table. "You see? Here's the little souvenir you gave me during our last meeting."

Sam glanced down at the familiar sight of his own business card. "Well, Mr. Reboul . . ."

"Please." Reboul waved a dismissive hand. "You must call me Francis, and I will call you Sam. More cozy, *non?*" He smiled and nodded, as though the idea of coziness were amusing. "I don't want to waste your time, so let me get to the point." He drank the last of his coffee and pushed his cup and saucer to one side with a manicured index finger. "In fact, the business that brings me to California is you."

Reboul paused for a moment and gave Sam a conspiratorial wink before continuing. "I have a situation in Marseille that requires someone—ideally, as you will see, an American—with particular and rather unusual gifts. And judging from our previous encounter, it seems to me that you would be just the man for the job. What would you say to a few weeks in Marseille? It's at its best this time of year, before the full heat of summer. I would make your stay extremely comfortable and, of course, very attractive financially."

Suspicion fought with curiosity, and curiosity won. "Let me guess." Sam returned Reboul's wink. "Would I be right in saying that what you have in mind is not altogether legal?"

Reboul frowned and shook his head, as though Sam had suggested something faintly improper. "Legality is so difficult, isn't it? If it were easier to define, most of the lawyers in the world would be out of business, which would be no bad thing. But my dear Sam, allow me to put your conscience at rest: I'm not proposing anything more illegal than a little harmless deception—and after your performance as a book publisher the last time we met, this would be child's play for a man of your talents. A mere *soupe de fèves,* as we say in Marseille." Reboul's attention suddenly shifted from Sam to the woman making her way through the garden toward their table. "How delightful," he said, smoothing his hair and standing up. "We have a visitor."

Sam turned to see Elena Morales, dressed in what she called her client uniform of black suit and black high heels, and carrying a slim black briefcase, the businesslike effect enlivened by a discreet flurry of black lace visible beneath the opening of her jacket. She stood over Sam, tapping her watch and looking far from pleased. "Is this your idea of casual Friday? Or have you forgotten about the meeting?"

"Ah," said Sam. "Right. The meeting. Give me five minutes to change, OK?" He was aware of Reboul hovering expectantly behind him. "Elena, this is Mr. Reboul." Elena smiled and offered her hand. "From Marseille," he added.

Reboul took Elena's hand as though it were a fragile object of immense value, and with a practiced swoop bent and kissed it. "*Enchanté, mademoiselle, enchanté.*" He gave the hand a second kiss. Sam resisted the urge to tell Reboul not to talk with his mouth full.

"If you two will excuse me," he said, "I'll be back as soon as I've slipped into my bulletproof vest."

Reboul pulled out a chair for Elena. "How pleasant it is to meet you. Forgive me for making Sam late, but I must have surprised him. The last time we met was in Marseille, and I don't think he expected to see me again."

"I'm sure he didn't. I know all about what happened in Marseille—he told me," said Elena. "Actually, I hired him. I'm with Knox, the insurance company."

"So you are business colleagues?"

"Now and then. But we're also . . . friends. You know?"

Reboul's eyes twinkled. "Lucky man. Perhaps you could help me persuade him to take on this little job for me. Even better—perhaps you would come with him." He patted her hand. "That would give me great pleasure."

Elena was aware that Reboul was out to charm her. She was aware, too, that she was rather enjoying it. "Where is this little job?"

"Marseille. It's a fascinating city. Let me tell you about it."

When Sam returned to the table, his bathrobe exchanged for a suit and tie, he found Reboul and Elena in animated conversation. It was his turn to stand over Elena, tapping his watch and looking smug.

Elena looked him up and down and grinned. "Very smart. Pity you forgot the socks, but that doesn't matter. We'd better go. Where did you leave the car?" Turning to Reboul, she said, "We'll see you back here this evening, then. In the restaurant at 7:30?"

Reboul inclined his head. "I shall count the moments."

Sam waited until they had joined the traffic on Sunset to head over to Wilshire before he spoke. "So what's happening this evening?"

"Francis is taking us to dinner, so he can tell us all about the job."

"Us?"

"He invited me to Marseille. And I'm tempted. More than that—I'd really like to go. I have a load of vacation time due, I've never been to the south of France, and Marseille . . ."

". . . is at its best this time of year." Sam pulled over to pass the bright pink Hummer dawdling along in front of him. "He doesn't waste any time, does he?"

"He's cute. And such a gentleman. You know something? I've never had my hand kissed before."

"It's against U.S. health and hygiene regulations." Sam shook his head. He knew from past experience that Elena was blessed with a whim of iron: once she had made a decision it was pointless trying to change her mind. And besides, he had to admit that having her with him would make the job a great deal more fun—if he decided to take it.

Meanwhile, they had the meeting to get through, and that certainly wasn't going to be fun. They were seeing Danny Roth to tie up the loose ends remaining from the recovery of his stolen wine and its shipment back to the States. There was also the matter of Sam's substantial finder's fee. Even though this was to be shared between Roth and Knox Insurance, Sam anticipated trouble: reluctance to pay at best, outrage and refusal more likely. He pulled up outside the tinted glass cube that was the headquarters of Roth and Partners (those being his mother and his accountant) and cut the engine. "Are you ready for this? Don't expect too much hand-kissing."

They were met in the reception area by Roth's executive secretary, the tall, regal, and incompetent Cecilia Volpé, who retained her job thanks to her influential father, Myron, one of the handful of powerful, anonymous men who ran Hollywood behind closed doors.

Cecilia swayed toward them on four-inch heels, brushing her mane of tawny hair from her forehead, the better to run her eye over Elena's outfit. "Love the shoes," she murmured. "Louboutin?" And then, remembering her duties, "Mr. Roth has a *very* busy schedule today. Will you be long?"

Sam shook his head and smiled. "Just as long as it takes to write a check."

Cecilia considered Sam's reply for a moment before deciding it was not to be taken seriously. She returned his smile, revealing several thousand dollars' worth of exquisitely capped teeth. "If you'd like to follow me?" She turned and swayed off down the corridor, her skirt clinging to a pair of buttocks, toned to perfection, that seemed to have a life of their own, twitching with every step. Sam was mesmerized.

Elena's elbow dug into his ribs. "Under no circumstances are you to make any comment. Keep your mind on your work."

Cecilia left them at the doorway of Roth's office. He was sitting with his back to them, the dome of his hairless head gleaming in the sunlight that flooded the room. He swiveled around, taking the phone from his ear, and looked at them through narrowed, unfriendly eyes. "Will this take long?"

"I hope not, Mr. Roth." Elena sat down and took some papers from her briefcase. "I know you have a very busy schedule. But there are one or two matters that we need to clear up."

Roth jerked his head toward Sam. "What's he doing here?"

"Me?" said Sam. "Oh, I've just come to pick up my check."

Roth assumed a shocked expression. "Check? Check? Sure you don't want a goddamn medal as well? Jesus."

Elena sighed. "The finder's fee, Mr. Roth. It's here in the insurance contract."

And there they stayed for almost two hours while Roth picked his way through the contract, line by line, disputing all but the most harmless clauses, his behavior just this side of apoplectic.

When they were finally through, Cecilia was summoned to escort them to the elevator. "Wow," she said, "he normally doesn't spend that much time with *anyone*. He must really like you guys."

Elena turned up the air-conditioning in the car and settled back in her seat. "If I needed another excuse to get out of town, that was it. The man's a monster. I'll tell you something—Marseille's looking better and better."

"Well, let's see what Reboul has to say."

"Don't even think of turning him down. I'll twist one arm, and he can twist the other." She leaned across and kissed Sam's ear. "Resistance will be useless."

# Two

Elena and Sam were late as they hurried along the corridor toward the elevator that would take them down to the Chateau Marmont restaurant and dinner with Francis Reboul.

They had been delayed by Elena's competitive urge, a desire to wear something that, in her words, would show Reboul that French women weren't the only babes in the world. After several false starts and considerable discussion, she had chosen a dress that was very much the style of the moment: black, tight, and short.

As they waited for the elevator to arrive, Sam put his arm around her waist, then allowed his hand to slide gently down to the upper slopes of the finely proportioned Morales *derrière*. His hand stopped, moved farther down, stopped again.

"Elena," he said, "are you wearing anything under that dress?"

"Not a lot," she said. "A couple of drops of Chanel." She

looked up at him and smiled her most innocent smile. "It's that kind of dress, you know? There's only room for me."

"Mmm." Sam was saved from further comment as the elevator doors opened to reveal a man wearing a blazer and brick-red trousers, with matching brick-red face. He was holding a half-empty martini glass, which he raised to them. "Going to a party out there in the garden," he said. "I thought I'd get some practice in first." As the elevator came to a stop, he drained his glass, put it in his blazer pocket, straightened his shoulders, and set off, weaving slightly.

Reboul was already at their table, champagne bucket at his elbow, going through a sheaf of papers. At the sight of Elena he leaped to his feet and took her hand, confining himself this time to a single kiss and a murmured *"Ravissante, ravissante."* Elena inclined her head prettily. Sam rolled his eyes. Their waiter poured champagne.

Reboul was a man for whom the word dapper might have been invented. Tonight he was resplendent in a black silk suit (the tiny scarlet ribbon of the Légion d'Honneur a nick of color on his lapel) and a shirt of the palest blue. A dazzling white handkerchief, also silk, was tucked into the cuff of his jacket. Like many fortunate Mediterranean men, his skin welcomed the sun, and his smooth, light-mahogany complexion provided a most flattering contrast with his perfectly white, perfectly trimmed hair. Even his eyebrows, Elena noticed, had received the skilled attentions of a master barber. Beneath the eyebrows, his brown eyes twinkled with good humor. He was living testimony to the joys of being rich. "A toast," he said, lifting his glass. "To the success of our little venture."

Sam paused, his glass halfway to his mouth. "I don't want to spoil the fun," he said, "but I like to know a lot more about my little ventures before I get too excited."

"And so you shall, my dear Sam, and so you shall." Reboul passed the wine list across to Sam. "But first, could I ask you to choose some wine for us? I seem to remember that you have an eye for a good vintage." This was accompanied by a raised eyebrow and a conspiratorial nod of the head, as though Reboul were sharing a secret.

It was the first time he had referred—albeit not too directly—to Sam's theft of several hundred bottles of the wines he had taken such trouble to acquire. And from his air of general benevolence, and the smile on his face, he appeared to find the incident amusing. Was that really how he felt? Perhaps now was not the moment, thought Sam, to pursue the subject. Without looking at the wine list, he pushed it to one side. "I hope you don't mind," he said, "but I've already arranged the wine. I have a little cellar here, unfortunately nothing like yours, and I chose one or two bottles you might find interesting. There's a Châteauneuf-du-Pape—but a *white* Châteauneuf-du-Pape—and one of our local wines you may not have tried yet: the Beckstoffer Cabernet from Napa. How do they sound?"

Reboul looked up from the menu. "*Formidable*. And now, dear Elena, what should I eat? Women always know best. I am in your hands."

Elena patted his arm. "Leave it to me." She studied the menu for a few moments. "*Soupe au pistou?* Maybe not—I guess you get plenty of that at home. The seafood is very good here, so you could start with crab cakes and a purée of avocado . . ."

Reboul held up his hand. "Say no more. I have a passion for crab cakes. I would kill for crab cakes."

"Let's hope that won't be necessary." Elena looked up from the menu. "What are we today? Tuesday? Great—the special today is braised rabbit and pappardelle with wild mushrooms. Delicious. Trust me."

"You amaze me," said Reboul. "I didn't know Americans ate rabbits."

"This American does."

The orders were placed, the bottles were uncorked, the champagne was given due attention, and, with a shrug of apology to Elena for bringing business to the table, Reboul started to outline the reason for his visit.

"Marseille is an extraordinary city," he began. "It was established more than twenty-six hundred years ago, before Paris was even called Paris. And it's big. The Marseille of today covers twice as much land as Paris. But, as you would imagine, the land along the coast of Marseille—land, as we say, with its feet in the Mediterranean—has almost all been developed." Reboul paused to take a sip of champagne. "Except for one charming little bay, the Anse des Pêcheurs, to the east of the old port. I won't bore you with the history of why it was never developed, except to say that for a hundred and twenty years it has been fought over and disputed by generations of city politicians and construction companies. There have been bribes, counter-bribes, court cases, and, so they say, at least one killing. But two years ago, at last, a decision was made to develop the Anse des Pêcheurs. It is a project very close to my heart, and I have already spent a great deal of time and money on it, but . . ."

The arrival of the crab cakes caused Reboul to stop, tuck a napkin into his shirt collar, try the white Châteauneuf, and compliment Sam on his choice.

"Tell me," asked Sam, "what happened to help all these guys finally make up their minds after a hundred and twenty years?"

Reboul took a longer, more considered sip of the Châteauneuf, holding it in his mouth and nodding his approval before replying. "Back in 2008, Marseille was voted European Capital of Culture for 2013, with the aim, to use the official language, of 'accelerating development.' I think that was the final push. At any rate, bids and ideas for developing the Anse were invited, and eventually a shortlist was drawn up of three proposals. One of them—the best, in my opinion—is mine. Also, my two competitors suffer from a disadvantage: they are foreigners, a group from Paris and an English syndicate. Neither of them has shown any imagination. Both want to build big hotels with all the modern trimmings—rooftop pools, spas, luxury shopping malls, the same tired old ideas. Fine for tourists, maybe, but not so good for the people who live in Marseille. And the buildings will undoubtedly be ugly concrete-and-glass boxes." He wiped the last of the avocado puree from his plate with a piece of bread and dabbed at his mouth with his napkin.

"We have a few of those here in L.A.," said Elena. "So what's your idea?"

"Ah," said Reboul, "something for the Marseillais. Apartments—but low, nothing higher than three floors—set in a terraced garden leading down to the sea. And then, a small marina, not for yachts but for the kind of little boats that ordinary people who live by the sea might have. I can show you the scale model of the project when we get to Marseille." He looked from Sam to Elena, his eyebrows raised. "*Et voilà*. What do you think?"

"Sounds a lot better than concrete boxes." Sam grinned. "But I have a feeling there might be more to this than architecture." He leaned back as the waiter arrived with their main course.

Reboul sighed. "Just so. There is a problem." He looked down at the plate that had been placed in front of him, and lowered his head for a closer inspection, inhaling deeply. "But before I explain, let us deal with this excellent rabbit."

The excellent rabbit was duly dealt with, the Beckstoffer Cabernet tasted, admired, and tasted again, and the conversation drifted pleasantly from winemaking to the charms of Cassis (Marseille's neighborhood vineyard) and on to the latest bee in Elena's bonnet. She had recently completed a wine course, and had been subjected by the rather patronizing instructor to the overblown vocabulary so beloved by wine experts.

"I'm sure the guy knew his stuff," she said. "And I can just about put up with pencil shavings and truffle oaks and hints of tobacco—although God knows who would want to drink pencil shavings—but I gave up when he started talking about wet dogs." She looked at Reboul, her dark eyes wide with mock horror. "You don't have wines that taste like wet dogs, do you?"

Reboul shook his head and laughed. "I once heard a wine-maker describe his wine as *'Comme le petit Jésus en pantalon de velours'*—like Jesus in velvet trousers." He shrugged. "Wine-makers are great enthusiasts. One must forgive their little exaggerations, I think. They are trying to describe something that is often indescribable."

The cheese arrived—three different cheeses, in fact—with a generous dollop of fig jam, and Reboul returned to his proposal. "There is, as I said, a problem, and his name is Patrimo-nio. Jérôme Patrimonio. He is the chairman of the committee that will choose the winning project, and as chairman he has, of course, more than just the influence of his personal vote." Reboul rearranged the cheeses on his plate while he tried to collect his thoughts. "Patrimonio hates me. He would do any-thing to stop me from winning. Anything."

Elena was the first to ask the obvious question. "Forgive me, but what did you do to him? Why does he hate you?"

"Ah." Reboul shook his head and sighed. "There was a woman." He looked at Elena as if, between sophisticated adults, that should be sufficient explanation. "And such a woman, too." The distant memory brought a half-smile to his face. "A long time ago, it's true. But Patrimonio is Corsican." Again, the significant look. "He is proud, like all Corsicans. And he has a very long memory, like all Corsicans."

"Let me get this straight," said Sam. "You know that this guy, who hates your guts, is the chairman of the committee. And yet you still think you have a chance?"

"You must let me finish, Sam. Patrimonio doesn't know I'm involved. My name does not appear on any of the bid documents, and I was careful not to involve any French companies that could be easily checked. My proposal was officially put forward by Langer & Troost, a very old and discreet Swiss private bank, and Van Buren Partners, a firm of American architects owned by Tommy Van Buren, who is an old, close friend of mine; we were at Harvard together. It is the international marketing representative of Van Buren who will make the final presentation to the committee. And there, my dear Sam, is where I hope you will make your appearance."

"As an architect who knows nothing about architecture? And an American, a foreigner, as well?" Sam shook his head. "I don't know, Francis. I think I may be short of a few qualifications."

Reboul disposed of such trifling concerns with a flick of his hand. "At this stage, it is not necessary to have any great knowledge of architecture. That will come later. But at the moment, we're selling an idea: somewhere for people to live, not just somewhere for them to visit. Something unique to Marseille, that respects the environment, that exists in harmony with the sea . . ."

Sam held up his hand. "OK. That could work. It's a nice, straightforward pitch. But why me? Why not have someone from Van Buren do it?"

Reboul leaned back, spreading his arms wide, a smile on

his face. "I need someone special—a top-class salesman; persuasive, charming, tactful. Which is exactly what you were in your previous career as a publisher. Remember?" He inclined his head toward Sam. "You fooled me. You could fool them."

Sam finished the wine in his glass and let Reboul pour some more. "Even though I'm a foreigner?"

"But Sam, there are foreigners and foreigners." Reboul held up one finger. "In Marseille, we have loathed Parisians for centuries. It's in our blood." He held up a second finger. "The English we tolerate. But since France is only separated from them by the Channel, they are a little too close, and they tend sometimes to get underfoot." He held up a third finger. "The Americans we like, not only for their many virtues, but also because America, most conveniently, is a long way away. So I think my project starts with a slight advantage."

Elena had been watching the exchange closely, as though it were a tennis match, her head going back and forth. "Let's assume your project wins," she said to Reboul. "Isn't it going to be a little difficult for you to stay out of it? Where's the money coming from? I mean, won't there be all kinds of performance guarantees and disclosures of interest—or are these just quaint old American customs?"

Reboul had been nodding while Elena spoke. "A very good point, my dear. Let me tell you how I intend to take care of it." He signaled the waiter and ordered coffee and Calvados for the three of them. "I have deposited sufficient funds with Troost & Langer—from an account in Dubai, so that nothing is seen to originate in France—to cover the first stages of construction. Once these have been carried out and the proj-

ect is well under way, there will be an unforeseen and totally
unexpected cash-flow problem." His eyes opened wide, his
mouth made an *O* of shocked surprise. "But fortunately, all
will be not lost. Help will be at hand, in the form of a sympathetic local investor. He will step in and, for the greater good
of Marseille, he will take over the financial responsibilities of
finishing the project."

"That will be you," said Elena.

"That will be me."

"And at that stage, there will be nothing Patrimonio can
do."

"Not a thing."

"So far, so good. All we need now is the salesman." Elena
turned to Sam. "Over to you, big boy."

Sam was outnumbered, and he knew it. He knew also that
if he turned down the job he risked incurring the disappointment and wrath of Elena, deprived of her first-ever vacation in
the South of France. Based on his past experience of Elena with
her blood up, this was a most disagreeable prospect. Besides,
a presentation such as Reboul had outlined was something he
could do standing on his head. And the trip might be fun.

"You win," he said. He raised his glass first to Elena, then
to Reboul. "A toast: here's to the success of our little venture."

A beaming Reboul leaped up and darted around the table.
*"Bravo!"* he said. *"Bravo!"* And promptly kissed the startled
Sam on both cheeks.

# Three

There are no crowds. There is no waiting in line. There are no surly security guards. There are no bags to juggle, no seating disputes, no neighbors with uncontrollable elbows and contagious ailments, no hysterical infants, no fetid, overworked toilets—in fact, flying by private jet deprives the passengers of all the familiar joys of air travel in the twenty-first century. But there are consolations, as Elena and Sam were discovering.

Reboul's Gulfstream G550 had been extravagantly reconfigured to carry no more than six passengers, two pilots, and a flight attendant in surroundings that Reboul liked to describe as *luxe et volupté*. The cabin was decorated in soothing tones of caramel and cream, with armchairs—one couldn't insult them by calling them mere seats—upholstered in chocolate-brown suede. There was a small dining area. Presiding over the tiny kitchen and bar at the front of the cabin was Mathilde, a handsome woman of a certain age, beautifully turned out in Saint Laurent and alert to the slightest signs of thirst and hunger. Passengers could stay in touch with the world below by phone and Internet; or relax with a library of current American and European films, to be watched on a large, high-definition screen. Cigar smokers could smoke their cigars. It seemed to Elena and Sam, as they accepted chilled flutes of Krug from Mathilde, that Reboul had done everything possible to make flying civilized.

"I could get used to this very, very quickly," said Elena. She was looking clear-eyed and radiant—her pale-olive complexion glowing, her black hair glossy—and Sam congratulated himself on his decision to take the job.

"Vacations suit you," he said. "Why don't we do this more often? You work too hard. How can the insurance business compare with a trip to the glamorous South of France with an adoring, irresistible companion?"

Elena looked at him beneath raised eyebrows. "I'll let you know," she said. "First I have to find an irresistible companion."

"Ah," said Reboul's voice behind them, "*les amoureux*. Has Mathilde been looking after you?" He had come from the rear of the plane, where he had a miniature office, and he was carrying a bulky file. "You must forgive me," he said to Elena, "but I need to steal Sam away from you so that we can go over the presentation while we have the chance of some peace and quiet. Once we get to Marseille . . ." He shook his head. "Busy, busy, busy."

Elena settled back in her armchair and opened Sam's old, dog-eared copy of the Cadogan Guide to the South of France, a favorite of his because of its well-informed, comprehensive coverage, its literate prose, and its refreshing sense of humor. She turned to the section on Marseille, wondering if she would find anything to account for Reboul's claim that Marseille and Paris had been at each other's throats for hundreds of years. And there it was, in the historical introduction. After explaining that an independently minded Marseille, in search of permanent autonomy, had been infuriating Louis XIV for forty years, the introduction continues: "By 1660, the King had had enough, and opened up a great breach in Marseille's walls, humiliating the city by turning its own cannons back on itself." (The cannons had previously pointed out to sea to repel pirates and invaders, but Louis had obviously decided that the city's residents were a greater threat.) And that wasn't all. "The central authority installed by Louis was much more lax than the city had previously been about the issues crucial to the running of a good port—like quarantine. The result, in 1720, was a devastating plague that spread throughout Provence."

So there was Marseille, menaced by its own guns and riddled with disease, all thanks to Parisian interference. Souvenirs like that stay in the memory for a long time, often becoming increasingly bitter from generation to generation. Reboul's comment, which Elena had at first dismissed as exaggeration, now made more sense.

She let the book slip to her lap, and looked out of the window at the pale-blue infinity of the evening sky, cloudless and calm. The pilot, in the delightfully accented English that he must have learned at pilot's charm school, had announced that with the help of the steady tail wind from west to east they would be arriving in Marseille in time for a breakfast of croissants and *café au lait*. Elena sank back into her suede cocoon, half listening to the buzz of conversation coming from Reboul and Sam.

He had been quite right; she did work too hard, and quite soon now she would have to make up her mind between her business life and her personal life. Frank Knox, the founder of Knox Insurance, was anxious to retire, and he had told Elena that the job of CEO was hers if she wanted it. But did she really want to spend the next thirty years up to her neck in clients like Danny Roth? How would Sam fit into a life governed by meetings, sales conferences, too much travel, and interminable client lunches? What would she do if she didn't take the job? With a shift of mental gears, she made herself think about the imminent pleasures of the next two to three weeks—Mediterranean beaches, entire days without schedules, and long, relaxed dinners under the stars. She dozed and dreamed.

Sam woke her by stroking her forehead with the tips of his fingers. "You were smiling," he said.

"I was on vacation," she said.

"Sorry to interrupt. But Francis thinks we might like to eat. He's invited us to what he calls a *pique-nique*."

Elena realized that packing—always, for her, a long and complicated business involving many refinements and changes of mind—had caused her to skip lunch. "I think I could force something down," she said. "Actually, I'm starving."

Mathilde had laid the dining table with white linen and cloth napkins and crystal glasses. A white orchid drooped elegantly from its vase, also crystal. It only needed Reboul in a chef's hat to complete the picture of a *restaurant de luxe*. In fact, he was in his working clothes: no jacket, no tie, the top two buttons of his silk shirt undone. Elena's eye was caught by what she at first took to be a monogram on his shirt pocket; a closer look showed it to be a line of tiny Chinese characters. Reboul noticed her interest and anticipated her question.

"These shirts are made for me in Hong Kong," he said. "Monsieur Wang, who makes them, likes to have his little joke, so he puts this on"—he tapped his chest—"instead of my initials. He told me it was a line from Confucius, ensuring a long life and good fortune."

"What does it say?"

"It says: Please take your hand off my left breast." Reboul shrugged and grinned. "Chinese sense of humor. Now then— what kind of picnic do you have for us, Mathilde?"

"There is smoked salmon. *Foie gras,* of course. The last of the asparagus." Mathilde paused here to kiss her fingertips. "Some good cheeses. And best of all, your favorite, Monsieur Francis: *salade tiède aux fèves et lardons.*" She waited, smiling, for Reboul's response.

"Oh!" he said. "Oh! I am dead and in heaven. Elena,

Sam—do you know this dish? A *warm* salad of young broad beans and chopped bacon? No? You must try it, and then we can attack the *foie gras* or the salmon. Or both. It has been an eternity since lunch." He turned to peer into the large ice bucket that Mathilde had placed on the bar. "You can stay with champagne, or we have an '86 Puligny-Montrachet and, for the *foie gras*, an '84 Sauternes. You must forgive me," he said to Elena, "but I never ask red wine to fly with me. The changes in altitude, the turbulence—they tend to upset even the best Bordeaux and Burgundy. I hope you understand."

Elena nodded knowledgeably, despite the fact that her wine course hadn't covered drinking on private jets. "Of course," she said, smiling sweetly. "But perhaps you could tell me more about this salad. I've never heard of it."

"My mother used to make it, and I learned from her. To start with, you take a saucepan of cold water, and a frying pan. Chop a large piece of fat bacon into cubes, and put them in the frying pan over medium heat. While they are cooking, put the beans into the saucepan of cold water, over high heat. The second the water comes to the boil, drain it off; the beans are ready. Put them into a bowl, and pour over them the chopped bacon—and, most important, every drop of hot bacon fat. *Et voilà*. Mix well and eat instantly, before the salad cools. It is sublime. You will see."

It was indeed sublime, as was everything else, and as Elena watched Reboul tuck into his salad, a plate of asparagus, and two thick slices of *foie gras*, she wondered how he managed to stay so trim. It was something she had asked herself last time she'd been to Paris and had been struck by the absence of obesity. The restaurants were full, the French ate and drank like champions, and yet most of them never seemed to put on weight. Unfair and mysterious.

"Why is it, Sam?"

"What?"

"Why don't the French get fat?"

Sam had asked the same question of Sophie, his accomplice in the wine robbery. Her answer had been delivered with the total conviction that came from having been born French, and thus having superior logic and common sense on her side, not to mention centuries of correct eating habits. Sam had no difficulty remembering her exact words: "We eat less than you do, we eat more slowly than you do, and we don't eat between meals. Simple."

While Elena was digesting these words of wisdom, Reboul joined in, shaking his head. "It's changing in France," he said. "Our habits are changing, our diet is changing, our shape is changing—too much fast food, too many sugary drinks." He patted his stomach. "Maybe I should give up Sauternes. But not just yet."

They were now flying into the darkness of night, and Mathilde had transformed their armchairs into flat beds and dimmed the cabin lights. It had been a hectic day for Elena and Sam, and they left Reboul, with a final glass of Sauternes, to catch up on his phone calls.

Elena yawned and stretched and lay back with a grateful sigh. She turned off her reading light. After two years without a vacation, she allowed the thought of tomorrow to wash over her. She would be in the South of France, with nothing to do but relax.

"Sam?"

"What?"

"Thanks for taking the job. You know, we should do this more often."

Sam smiled in the darkness. "Goodnight, Elena."

"Goodnight, Sam."


Mathilde, crisp and fresh and dressed by Saint Laurent in the colors of the French flag—red silk scarf, white shirt, and blue suit—woke them with the offer of orange juice, croissants, and coffee. They would be landing in half an hour. The sun was already up and, according to the pilot's cheerful report, the weather forecast promised a fine warm day with temperatures in the high seventies.

They were finishing breakfast when Reboul appeared, perky and newly shaved, to have a cup of coffee with them. After being assured that they had slept well, he moved a little closer to Sam and lowered his voice. "Once we're in Marseille," he said, "it is important that we're not seen together. That would risk spoiling everything. So when we land, I shall stay on the plane for half an hour to let you get away. Your car and your driver, Olivier, are waiting for you. He will take you to the house where you will be staying. Claudine will meet you there and take care of everything you need. She will give you each a cell phone with a French number. Call me—you'll find my cell number in your phone memory—to make sure we can be in touch at any time. And then, well . . ." Reboul made an expansive gesture in the general direction of the city. "Marseille is yours for the day. I can recommend Peron for lunch, or Olivier can take you to Cassis, Aix, the Luberon, wherever you like. Work starts tomorrow. Let's talk this evening to go over the details."

They were now starting their descent, and Elena had her first glimpse of the Mediterranean, glinting in the sun, with the outer limits of the sprawl of Marseille visible in the distance. She reached over and took Sam's hand. "Isn't the light fantastic? Everything looks like it's been scrubbed. Where's the smog?"

Sam squeezed her hand. "Homesick already? I don't think they do smog here. The mistral keeps it away—or maybe it's the garlic in the *bouillabaisse*. You're going to like Marseille; it's a fine old town. Shall we stay here today, or do you want to see a bit of the coast?"

Before Elena could reply, Mathilde came by to check their seat belts and go over the landing procedure. "All you need are your passports," she said. "Your bags will be cleared through customs and put in the car. Olivier will be waiting in the parking area. I hope you have a wonderful stay in Marseille."

The plane touched down and taxied toward the small private terminal before easing to a halt. Not quite like landing at LAX, Elena thought, as she watched the baggage handlers scurrying around the plane. She half expected to be picked up bodily and carried by careful hands for the final short leg of the journey.

They made their farewells to Reboul, Mathilde, and the pilot, and stepped out into a glorious Provençal morning—sharp, polished light and a high, thick blue sky. There was a brief stop at immigration, where the officer welcomed them to France, and then through the terminal doors. Fifty yards away, a long, black Peugeot and a young man in a suit were waiting. He held the door open for Elena, showed Sam the luggage in the trunk, and then they were off. The time between leaving the plane and getting into the car had been just over five minutes.

"I'm running out of nice things to say," said Elena, shaking her head. "But I know what I'd like for Christmas."

# Four

The big Peugeot made its cautious way through the cramped streets of Marseille's 7th and 8th arrondissements, where the great and the good—and the chic have their homes. Olivier was driving at walking pace and often had only inches to spare. He was negotiating the narrow, twisting Chemin du Roucas Blanc, passing between high walls that half concealed villas built in the pompous style greatly admired by the prosperous merchants of the nineteenth century. Occasionally there would be an architectural hiccup: a modern white ranch house looking slightly uncomfortable so far from California, or a tiny, shabby building, little more than a hut, which had once sheltered a fisherman and his family. This was typical of Marseille, Olivier said: wealth and poverty cheek by jowl, palaces next to hovels—the marks of a city that had grown organically, without much interference from urban planners.

As they drew closer to the sea, the walls on either side

seemed to become higher, and the houses bigger. These had been built here by the richest merchants of Marseille not only for the beauty of the sea views, but so that they could keep an eye on their floating assets — the ships and their delightfully profitable cargoes going in and out of the port.

"Wow," said Elena. "See that place? What a spot." They had come to the brow of a rise in the road, and she was looking at a house just below them. It was built on a point that jutted out toward the sea, surrounded by a small forest of parasol pines, and protected by the inevitable high wall.

Olivier was smiling. "Monsieur Reboul hopes you will find it comfortable. This is where he used to live before he moved to Le Pharo. You won't be disturbed here. It's very peaceful." He slowed down to give the iron gates time to swing open, and pulled up on the gravel forecourt in front of a short flight of steps that led to the massive entrance door.

Waiting at the top of the steps was a welcoming committee of two: a slim, elegant figure with short, gray hair, and a much larger, younger woman whose wide, white smile was perfectly set off by her shining black face. Olivier introduced them as Claudine, who ran the house, and Nanou from Martinique, who was the maid. "Claudine's English is excellent," said Olivier, "but with Nanou it is what I think you call a work in progress." At the sound of her name, Nanou took a deep breath. "How you doing?" she said, followed by "Have a nice day," and then spoiled the effect by dissolving into giggles.

Claudine led them into the house, across a gleaming expanse of beeswaxed herringbone parquet, up a broad stair-

case, and through double doors into what was to be their bedroom.

Sam looked around and let out a low whistle. "I guess we'll
be able to squeeze in here," he said. "It's about the same size
as my apartment."

Claudine smiled. "It used to be Monsieur Reboul's bedroom." She pointed to two doors set into the far wall. "You
each have a bathroom. Monsieur Reboul always says that
the secret of a harmonious relationship between a man and a
woman is to have separate bathrooms."

"Amen," said Sam. There was a muffled snort from Elena.

"I'll leave you to unpack. Then perhaps you'd like coffee
on the terrace. I can give you your phones and answer any
questions you may have."

Elena had been making a tour of inspection that took in
the closet space (capacious, even by American standards), the
bathrooms (vast, marbled, and well lit), the four-poster bed
(for its degree of firmness and bounce), and the views through
the long windows. "Sam, what is that on the hill over there?
There's something shiny on the top. Looks wonderful."

Sam went over and stood behind her, massaging the back
of her neck while he studied the view to the northeast. In
the distance he could see the massive basilica which he had
come to know on his previous visit to Marseille. He cleared
his throat and assumed his most professorial voice. "That is
Notre-Dame de la Garde, constructed in the neo-Byzantine
style, and crowned by a golden statue of the Virgin. She is
over thirty feet high, and known locally as 'La Bonne Mère,'

greatly loved for her miraculous qualities. In the tower is a bell that weighs eight tons. The bell is called Marie-Joséphine. The clapper is called Bertrand. The . . ."

"Sam, you're full of it." She gave him a peck on the cheek. "I'm going to take a quick shower, and you could do with a shave."

Fifteen minutes later, showered and changed, they were sitting with Claudine on the terrace. Below them, the sea, glittering in the sun, was dotted with sailing boats. On the low wall of the terrace, two seagulls were conducting a raucous squabble over a withered morsel of something mysterious and long dead.

"Look at those guys," said Elena. "They're huge. They're like turkeys."

Claudine poured coffee. "If you believe what you hear, we also have sardines the size of sharks. Everything in Marseille is bigger, and if it's not, we pretend it is. I think it is like your Texas, *non?*" She smiled and shook her head. "Now then. Here are your phones, each with four names in the memory: Monsieur Reboul, Olivier, myself, and, of course, you have each other's numbers in there. Monsieur Reboul asks that you call him sometime today to check that everything is OK. Here are some business cards for Monsieur Levitt, identifying him as vice president of Van Buren Partners. And here is a member's pass to the Cercle des Nageurs, the swimming club. It has an Olympic-sized pool and a nice restaurant, which is very agreeable for lunch. And finally, when you have finished your coffee, perhaps we can go inside and see the project model that will be used at the presentation."

The model had been set up in the dining room, taking up most of the long oak table, and it precisely matched Reboul's earlier description of a low, crescent-shaped range of apartments overlooking a garden that led to a marina. Sam was immediately struck by the attention to detail, even down to the colors of the shutters and the miniature residents strolling between tiny trees in the garden or having a nautical moment among their tiny boats in the marina. The only thing missing, he thought, was a snug little bar overlooking the sea. But on the whole, he was very pleased with what he saw. It would fit in with the coastline, it wouldn't add an ugly concrete stump to the skyline, and it would provide homes for hundreds of Marseillais. Reboul's architect friend had done well.

Sam was wondering what it would be like to live there when Elena called out across the room. "Don't forget this is a vacation day. Claudine thinks we'd like Cassis, and Olivier's waiting outside to take us. How about it?"


"This is the life," said Elena, adjusting her sunglasses and leaning back in her seat as the car crept back down the Chemin du Roucas Blanc. Cassis was only thirty kilometers away, the sun was high in the sky, and she hadn't thought about the office all morning. "Somebody once said that it takes you years to accept hardship and bad luck, but only twenty-four hours to get used to comfort and good luck. Chauffeurs, housekeepers, maids—I love it."

It showed. The last time Sam had seen her this relaxed had been during a few days they had stolen in Paris. He was beginning to think that the very fact of being in France was enough to lift her spirits—no doubt helped by the thousands of miles of separation from the insurance business. If Olivier hadn't been sitting inches away, he would have suggested an idea he'd been keeping to himself for some time: a divided life, with summers in Provence and winters in L.A. Maybe he'd bring it up when the moment was right.

"You know," he said, "you're fluent in Spanish. You'd pick up French very fast."

Elena gave him a sideways look. "Is this leading somewhere?"

Sam smiled, but didn't answer. Ever since their last explosive breakup and reconciliation, each of them had been careful to avoid talking about the future. Although Elena spent most nights with Sam at the Chateau Marmont, she still kept her apartment, her job, and her independence. At the moment this suited her, but for how much longer?

"Well, you know me, Sam. Always open to an interesting offer." She fluttered her eyelashes at him, then realized that the fluttering was in vain, as she was wearing Hollywood-size sunglasses.

Sam fished in his pocket for his phone. "Do you want to say hello to your favorite journalist? I thought we might have dinner with him tonight."

Philippe Davin had been one of the most pleasant surprises of Sam's previous trip to Marseille. A senior journalist for *La Provence,* the self-styled bible of Provençal news, Philippe had taken Sam under his well-informed wing in exchange for exclusive rights to any story that might develop. Better still, he had acted as driver of the getaway vehicle—an elderly plumber's van—when Sam had removed the wine from Reboul's cellar. To complete the assignment, Philippe had gone to Los Angeles to interview the legal owner of those bottles, Danny Roth, and it was then that he had met Elena.

To Sam's relief, the two of them had taken to one another instantly. Philippe scampered around Elena like a large, undisciplined puppy, calling her La Bomba Latina and keeping her amused with extravagant compliments and some woefully bad attempts at Spanish. In return, she was happy to give him what she called L.A. 101, a basic guide to the city's habits and diversions, and she found plenty to enjoy in his reactions. He loved the Lakers game they went to, but was completely bewildered by American football. Puzzled by the unnaturally placid behavior of Los Angeles drivers, stunned by the prices of modest wooden houses in Malibu, appreciative of the seemingly endless parade of young blondes, impressed by Californian wines, amazed at the agility of superannuated surfers—he was fascinated by it all. He suffered only two disappointments: there was no sign of former governor Schwarzenegger on Muscle Beach, and a visit to Starbucks passed without seeing anyone draw a gun. But otherwise the trip had been a great success, and he had made Elena promise to come to Marseille so that he could return the favor.

"Philippe? It's Sam. I'm here in town for a few days." He winced, and held the phone away from his ear to lessen the volume of Philippe's enthusiastic response.

"Listen—I'll tell you all about it when I see you. How about dinner tonight? Great. You choose somewhere and I'll call you back later. Meanwhile, I have one of your admirers here."

He passed the phone to Elena. There was a second explosion of joy from Philippe, followed by heated expressions of devotion that brought a blush to Elena's cheek. "Philippe," she said at last, cutting him off, "you are *so* bad. See you tonight. Can't wait."

They were dropping down toward Cassis now, passing some of the fastidiously maintained vineyards that produced the white wine considered by the gourmets of Marseille to be the only proper accompaniment for a *bouillabaisse*. Needless to say, the Marseillais had their own highly exaggerated account of how the wines of Cassis came into being, as Olivier explained.

In effect, so the story went, the vineyards were established by Le Bon Dieu. He came down from heaven one day and by chance saw a family working on the rocky slopes above Cassis. It was hard, backbreaking work, and nothing seemed to be growing. This made God very sad, and as He saw how the family suffered, He shed a tear. Miraculously, the tear fell on a struggling vine, which promptly started to flourish before giving birth to a wonderful—some would say divine—wine with a delicate tint of the palest green. The Provençal poet Frédéric Mistral found time between stanzas to enjoy the odd glass, and claimed to detect hints of heather, rosemary, and myrtle.

"We'll try a bottle with lunch," Sam said to Elena, "and you can amaze me with the sensitivity of your palate and the delicacy of your powers of description."

Normally, Elena never allowed sarcasm to pass unpunished, but this time she was far too busy taking in the view. Cassis is thought by many to be the prettiest spot on the coast. Apart from its vineyards, it has everything: a medieval citadel, cliffs, beaches, a charming port lined with cafés and restaurants, even a casino where the Marseillais go to lose their shirts.

Olivier dropped them off and pointed them in the right direction for the port. He, too, had a lunch date, with a girl from the village, and when he wished them *bon appétit*, he hoped they wouldn't hurry back. He had his mind on other things.

The port of Cassis, subject of a million postcards and the victim of innumerable bad amateur artists, is almost too picturesque to be true. It is small—a five-minute stroll takes you from one end to the other—and you are likely to see the occasional character, dressed in peaked cap and sleeveless vest, who might have escaped from one of Marcel Pagnol's books. Fishermen squat in their boats, scissors flashing in the sun, as they open sea urchins and suck out the nectar, middle-aged men with flamboyant moustaches sit in cafés plying young blond women with *coupes* of champagne, the small, brightly painted ferries come and go between the port and the narrow rocky inlets the locals call *calanques*, the air is clean and salty, and the sun casts a benevolent glow over it all. Work and the other harsh realities of life seem a million miles away.

Elena and Sam found a café table with an uninterrupted view of the passing parade. This, as Elena noticed with interest, was divided into two distinct groups that could be identified by what they were wearing. Tourists were dressed for high summer, even though it was only spring: women in flowing caftans, sandals, white sundresses, the odd cartwheel straw hat; men in T-shirts and rumpled shorts festooned with multiple bulging pockets (or, even worse, abbreviated camouflage-print trousers that ended six inches above the ankle). The local inhabitants, who clearly didn't trust the weather, were protected from possible snowstorms by sweaters or scarves, boots for the ladies, and leather jackets for the men. It was as though the passers-by were living in two different climates.

"My father likes to hunt," said Elena, "and he gets really mad if he sees deer or wild boar when he's left his rifle at home. 'Look at that,' he always says. 'The things you see when you haven't got your gun.' Well, now I know how he feels." She nodded in the direction of the quay, where a woman with unnaturally bright red hair was posing by a bollard while her companion fussed with his camera. The woman was well into her forties. She was wearing the shortest of shorts and the highest of high heels, and her bare legs had the pallor of flesh that had spent the winter under a stone. Nevertheless, she quite obviously had a high opinion of her appearance, flouncing around the bollard, tossing her radioactive curls, and renewing her lip gloss between each shot.

"When French women get it wrong they really get it wrong," Elena muttered, with considerable satisfaction.

They left the café and made their way through the slow drift of people until they came to the blue awning and flowered terrace that Sam remembered from his first visit to Cassis. "This is Chez Nino," he said. "Terrific fish and a view of the port. Wines from up there in the hills. You'll love it."

And so she did. For someone like Elena, whose usual lunch was cottage cheese and salad, eaten in a hurry at her desk, Nino was a sunny, self-indulgent revelation. They had *soupe de poissons,* the formidable Provençal fish soup, laced with *rouille,* a thick, garlic-loaded sauce. They had perfectly grilled scorpion fish. They had a bottle of *rosé* from the Domaine du Paternel.

They ordered coffee, and it was the moment to sit back and look around. The restaurant was full, and Elena was struck by the volume of laughter and boisterous conversation coming from the surrounding tables. "These guys make a lot more noise than Parisians," she said. "It must be something they put in the soup."

Sam considered the pleasing possibility that *soupe de poissons* could be a mood-enhancing substance, and had a brief vision of restaurant customers floating back to work after lunch high on fish soup. "Afraid not," he said. "Actually, I think it's in the genes. A lot of Provence used to be Italian. The popes were once based in Avignon. Nice was called Nizza. You look in the phone book, and you'll find Italian names on every page: Cipollina, Fachinetti, Onorato, Mastrangelo—there are thousands of them, and they add a lot to the atmosphere down here. It's one of the things I like about Provence; one of the things that makes it so different from northern France."

"Sam, you're turning into a walking guide book. I'm impressed. And you know something? I'm picking up local habits fast."

"Siesta?" said Sam. "You're in luck. I happen to know this is a restaurant with rooms."

Elena shook her head. "You can wipe that leer off your face. The thought of a siesta had never crossed my mind. Like any good Frenchwoman who's just finished a long lunch, what I really want to know is where we're going for dinner."

"Philippe's taking care of that. Don't worry. He'll make sure we don't starve tonight. Sure you don't want to check out those rooms?"

# Five

Sam could hear a few moments of Mozart in the background before Reboul's voice cut in.

"*Alors*, Sam. How was your day in Cassis?"

"Good, Francis. We had a great time. Elena loved it." Sam looked down at the notes he'd made on the back of Nino's lunch bill. "I wanted to go over a couple of points with you before we go out this evening. We're having dinner with a friend, Philippe Davin. He's a journalist with *La Provence*, and I'm hoping he can give me some background on Patrimonio and the distinguished members of the selection committee."

"A journalist?" Reboul's voice was less than enthusiastic. "Sam, are you sure . . ."

"Don't worry. I'll stick to the plot. Your name won't come into it. Now tell me—is there anything particular you're interested in? Philippe's a bloodhound. What he doesn't know he can usually sniff out."

"Well, whatever you can find out about the other two projects and the people behind them would be useful, but not the usual press release nonsense about their hobbies and their charitable donations. For instance, I'd love to know where they're getting their money from. Also, don't forget the personal side. Do they have debts? Addictions? Mistresses? A fondness for call girls? How do they stand with Patrimonio? Are there any rumors of bribery?" Reboul paused, and Sam could hear the click of a glass being put back on a table. "Not that I would dream of exploiting any of this, you understand."

"Of course not."

"But in business, information is like gold. You can't have too much of it."

"I'll bear that in mind, Francis."

"Have a pleasant evening, my friend. *Bon appétit.*"

Sam was smiling as he put down the phone. There had been a wistful note to Reboul's voice, and Sam had the feeling that he would have liked to join them for dinner.

They had arranged to meet Philippe at Le Bistrot d'Edouard on Rue Jean Mermoz, which Philippe had chosen as a tribute to Elena. It was a Latin restaurant, and so La Bomba Latina would feel instantly at home. Moreover, said Philippe, she would be ravished by the huge selection of *tapas*.

In fact it was Sam who was ravished first, as soon as they had come through the door. It looked like his kind of restaurant: a series of simple, intimate rooms, plain white paper tablecloths, the painted walls—oxblood-red below, white above—hung with blackboards listing the wines and the *tapas* of the day, the early arrivals with their jackets off and their napkins tucked into shirt collars, which was always a sign of healthy appetites and good food, and a smiling welcome from the girl behind the bar.

They were led up a short flight of stairs to a corner table on the first floor, where a beaming Philippe, ice bucket already loaded and poised, jumped to his feet and crushed Elena to his bosom. Compliments and cries of delight followed, and Sam, who was by now getting used to these expressions of masculine affection, received a kiss on each cheek. Finally, slightly out of breath, Philippe sat them down and poured each of them a glass of wine.

"This is a wonderful surprise," he said. "What are you doing here? How long are you staying? Where are you staying? But first, a toast." He raised his glass. "To friendship." He leaned back in his chair, still beaming, and gave Elena and Sam a chance to admire the adjustments he had made to his appearance since they had last seen him in Los Angeles.

Previously, he had favored a style of dress he liked to describe as "mercenary chic"—army-surplus pants and jackets, olive-drab fatigue caps, and paratrooper's boots. His black hair had been abundant, and undisturbed by the comb.

All this had gone, and Che Guevara had been replaced by Tom Ford. The new version of Philippe had a closely clipped head, the hair on his scalp very little longer than the dark, three-day stubble on his face. His clothes were razor-sharp: a skinny black suit and a whiter-than-white shirt, unbuttoned at the neck, with highly polished black shoes. He might have been a fashion-conscious soccer player or a refugee from the Cannes film festival, which was currently taking place farther along the coast.

"Notice anything different?" Philippe didn't give them time to reply. "I've changed *mon look*. Mimi at the office is now in charge of my personal presentation. What do you think?"

"Where are the sunglasses?" said Elena. "And how about an earring?"

"Where's the Rolex?" said Sam.

Philippe grinned, shot his cuffs, and there it was: a great stainless-steel carbuncle, guaranteed waterproof to a depth of a thousand feet.

Sam shook his head in wonder. "Congratulations to Mimi. She's turned you into a style icon. I hope you've kept the scooter."

"*Mais bien sûr*. It's the only way to get around Marseille. But enough of me—what are you two doing here?" He waggled his eyebrows energetically. "Honeymoon?"

"Not exactly," said Sam. And while they drank the Quatre Vents that Philippe had chosen because, as he said, of its *rondeur* and its shimmer of green, Sam gave him an edited version of his assignment: hired by an American architect, backed by Swiss money, in town to persuade the selection committee that a three-story apartment complex would suit Marseille better than a forty-floor hotel.

Philippe listened carefully, nodding from time to time. "I've been hearing all kinds of things about this," he said, "and I've been trying to set up interviews with your competitors, but they're acting very shy at the moment."

"Do you know who they are, anything about them?"

"OK." Philippe glanced around the room before adopting the investigative journalist's standard operating position—body tilted forward in a confidential crouch, head sunk into his shoulders, the voice low and discreet. "There are two other syndicates: one British, one French. Or perhaps I should say Parisian. The head Brit is Lord Wapping, an ex-bookmaker who bribed his way into the House of Lords with some heavy financial contributions to both of the major political parties."

"Both of them?"

"*Mais oui*. Apparently it happens all the time in England. It's what they call a win-win situation." Philippe paused for a sip of wine. "The leader of the Parisian project is a woman, Caroline Dumas. Very bright, very well connected politically, used to be a junior minister until she got too friendly with a senior minister and his wife found out. Now she works for Eiffel International; it's one of those huge conglomerates—construction, agribusiness, electronics, with a chain of hotels on the side. Personally, I don't think she has much of a chance on this one."

"Why not?"

"She's Parisian." Philippe shrugged. He clearly felt that, in Marseille, no further explanation was necessary.

Their waitress, who had been hovering patiently, took advantage of the gap in the conversation and directed their attention to the list of *tapas* on the blackboard.

That particular night in May there were fifteen to choose from: *pata negra* ham from acorn-fed pigs in Spain; tuna roe drizzled with olive oil; fried aubergines dusted with mint; tartare of salmon, with honey and dill; deep-fried zucchini flowers; clams; artichokes; monkfish; anchovies—a selection of delights that had them in agonies of indecision. They finally agreed on three *tapas* each, followed, at Philippe's insistence, by the specialty of the house: inkfish with blackened pasta.

Sitting back to take another look at her surroundings, Elena's eye was caught by a frieze of oversized handwriting that ran along the top of the wall just below the ceiling. The same three words—*buvez riez chantez*—were repeated around all the walls of the upstairs room.

"What is that?" she asked. "Some kind of weird French thing like a *tapas* code?"

"It means drink, laugh, sing," said Philippe. "To encourage us to have fun." A sudden roar of laughter from the next table interrupted him. "Not that we need much encouragement."

"I find it very strange," said Sam, "that the average Frenchman has this reputation for being . . . well, serious, you know? Not the kind of guy to let his hair down. Too concerned with appearances."

"What you call a tight-ass?" suggested Philippe.

Sam grinned. "I never said that. But actually, most of the French I've met love to have a good time. I remember going to the wine auctions in Beaune once and I couldn't keep up. Drinking, laughing, singing? That's all they did for three days straight. And yet there's this image of the straitlaced French. I don't get it."

Philippe held up his finger, a sure sign that enlightenment was to follow. "That's because people like to pigeonhole us, to take one aspect of our personality and judge us on that. Now, of course we are serious about important things—money and food and rugby, for instance. But we are more complex than that, and we are full of contrasts. On the one hand, we are amazingly egotistical: the two most popular words in the French language are *moi* and *je*, normally used together. And yet our treatment of others is usually polite, even considerate. We show respect. We kiss, we shake hands, we men rise to our feet for women, we leave the room when we take phone calls so as not to irritate people around us." He paused to take a long sip of wine. "We drink, my God how we drink. But it is very unusual to see public drunkenness. We dress conservatively, and yet French women led the world in going topless on the beaches. It has been said that our national preoccupations are sex, hypochondria, and the belly. But there is more to us than that." He nodded his approval of what he had just said, and held out the empty wine bottle to a passing waitress for a refill.

Elena had been paying close attention to this crash course in the French psyche, and, in what she hoped was true Gallic style, held up a finger of her own and wagged it. "Handshaking, OK. Cheek-kissing, OK. Polite, OK. Until they get into their cars. I have to tell you I have never seen so many seriously homicidal drivers as there are in France. What's their problem?"

Philippe smiled and shrugged. "Some would say *joie de vivre*, but I have another theory. I think that French drivers suffer from a physical disability: they only have two hands, when, of course, they need three. Smoking and the telephone take up one hand and the other must be kept free in order to make insulting gestures at other drivers who are too fast, too slow, too close, or Belgian." Seeing Elena's puzzled expression, he added, "Belgians always drive in the middle of the road. This is well known. Ah, here are the *tapas*."

The next few minutes passed in a contented semi-silence as they explored the nine small dishes set before them, sniffing, tasting, sometimes exchanging a forkful of violet-colored artichoke for a tender little clam wrapped in Spanish ham, or mopping up the herb-scented olive oil with their bread. In many ways, *tapas* make an ideal first course: not too heavy, with a variety of flavors to wake up the taste buds, and served in modest amounts that don't blunt the appetite. With the final dish wiped clean, the conversation returned to business.

"I guess you know there's some kind of press reception and cocktail party later on this week," Sam said to Philippe. "Are you going? Will Patrimonio be there?"

Philippe raised his eyes to the ceiling. "*Bof!* Try to keep him away. This is his moment of glory. I'm afraid we can expect a speech from the old windbag. I shall be there to record it for posterity. And you will have a chance to meet your competitors, take a look at their ideas." He shook his head at the thought. "Hotels, hotels, hotels. It's always hotels or office buildings."

"So what do you think of our idea?"

"Of course, I haven't seen the details. Even so, I hope it will win. It's more human, more civilized." Philippe stared into his wine glass, his expression thoughtful. "But from what I hear, Wapping has a history of always getting what he wants, one way or another. Not an easy man to beat. And you can usually trust Patrimonio to make the wrong decision."

Elena was frowning as she put down her glass. "You keep talking about Patrimonio as if he were the only guy that mattered. I know he's chairman, but isn't there a committee? Don't the members have a say? Or are they just dummies put there to make up the numbers?"

Philippe started to run his fingers through his hair—an old habit—until he realized that there was nothing left to run his fingers through. "There are six, or maybe seven, on the committee. I know that two of them owe their jobs to Patrimonio, so they'll vote the way he tells them to. As for the others, your guess is as good as mine. They'll all be at the reception. I'll see what I can find out."

The dish of the day arrived in all its dusky glory, with tendrils and thin slices of inkfish resting on a bed of glistening black angel's-hair pasta. To one side, for a change of texture, and to provide what Philippe called an epiphany for the palate, there was a creamy sauce of goat's cheese.

Elena took her first mouthful, and let out a small sigh of pleasure. "This is lovely. Is it going to give me black lips?"

Sam leaned forward to inspect her mouth. "Not yet. So far, it's just the teeth."

Elena turned to Philippe. "See what I have to put up with?"

Philippe nodded his head in sympathy. "Humor is how the Anglo-Saxon man declares his love," he said. "A Frenchman is . . . ," he performed a demi-shrug, with just the one shoulder cocked, "more subtle, more romantic, altogether more alluring."

"I like it," said Elena. "Alluring is nice."

Sam felt it was time to change the subject. "Tell us about Mimi at the office. Is this the real thing? Has she started redecorating your apartment? She's certainly redecorated you."

Philippe turned to Elena. "You see? He mocks me. Now then: what can I tell you about Mimi? Petite, red hair, highly intelligent, witty, wonderful legs, and, obviously"—here, he smirked—"excellent taste in men. You will adore her. She wanted to come tonight, but she has a martial-arts class."

Thoughts of Mimi gave way to consideration of dessert, with Philippe persuading Elena to try what he described as a *profiterole* on steroids, a veritable prince of *profiteroles,* plumped up with a miraculously light *crème Chantilly.* Sam contented himself with some Manchego cheese—sliced thin, the way it should be—with quince jam and a glass of solid red wine from the Languedoc. As he ate, he listened to Philippe describing to Elena a few of the city's distractions: the Cathédrale de la Major, supported by 444 marble columns; the Vieux Port; twentieth-century art in the Musée Cantini; Pagnol's Bar de la Marine; the magnificent Vieille Charité, designed by the court architect of Louis XIV to shelter the homeless; the view from Notre-Dame de la Garde. Or perhaps a tour of the boutiques, guided by Mimi, followed by a restorative session in the spa on the Corniche. And, of course, there was always Marseille's favorite blood sport.

"If you like soccer," said Philippe, "this is not to be

missed—Olympique de Marseille's last game of the season, against Paris Saint-Germain. We detest them. Mark my words, it will be a grudge match."

"Sounds interesting," said Elena. "What does a girl wear to a grudge match?"

"Body armor." Philippe took a deep, noisy breath through pursed lips. "Those PSG fans are brutes."

Over coffee, it was agreed that Elena and Mimi would meet the next day. Sam was to continue polishing up his presentation, and Philippe planned to call his contacts in the city bureaucracy to see what he could dig up. They said their farewells in the soft, warm darkness outside the restaurant. Philippe slipped on his sunglasses against the glare of the moon, cocked a leg over his scooter, and clattered off. Tomorrow would be a busy day for all of them.

# Six

Sam finished reading the last of the documents and sat back with a sigh of relief. He now knew enough—more than enough—about Reboul's development plans, from the number of berths in the marina to the color of the roof tiles and the size of the bathrooms. The next step would be to transform this mass of detail into a sixty-minute presentation for Patrimonio's committee. He stood up, stretched to ease his aching back, and pushed open the shutters to let in the sunlight. It was a beautiful blue and gold Mediterranean morning. He wondered how Elena and Mimi were getting on, and resisted the temptation to call Elena and invite himself to lunch. Work, he said to himself. That's what you're here for. Work.

He was saved from further self-improvement by his phone. It was Philippe, sounding furtive and conspiratorial.

"Can you talk?"

Sam wondered if he should check under the desk for eaves-droppers. "Sure. Go ahead."

"I have this contact who works in one of the bars on the Vieux Port. A man who keeps his eyes and ears open. Well, one of his friends does a little business in the summer with boats coming into Frioul—you know, those islands just off the coast. And guess who's been there for the past few days, in one of the hidden moorings."

Sam's mind ran the gamut from President Sarkozy to Brad Pitt. "I don't know, Philippe. You tell me."

"Lord Wapping. Interesting, *non?* And that's not all. Last night, he gave a dinner party on his yacht—which, incidentally, is called *The Floating Pound*. I'm told this is an English joke. And listen to this: Patrimonio was one of his dinner guests."

"Why am I not surprised?" said Sam. "I'd better tell my partners. Maybe they can arrange to have Wapping shot."

There was a snort of irritation from Philippe. "Always the jokes. But I tell you—an intimacy like this is not good news. Anyway, I think we should go out and take a look at the boat. It would be an interesting detail for my piece."

"Your piece?"

"Actually, it's a series I'm doing for the paper. I'm calling it 'The Diary of a Development.' Here—I'll read you the first paragraph." He cleared his throat and assumed the weighty, sonorous tone of a television newsreader.

" 'The Anse des Pêcheurs, for countless centuries a tranquil refuge for the fishermen of Marseille, will shortly undergo a total transformation. Just what form this transformation will take is to be decided over the coming weeks by a development committee under the chairmanship of Jérôme Patrimonio, for many years a prominent figure in city affairs. The committee will be considering three competitive projects, and in our exclusive series we shall be examining these projects—and the organizations behind each one—so that you, our readers, will be fully informed about the most significant change to the Marseille coastline in generations.' "

Philippe's voice returned to normal. "It's a pretty standard opening, but I'll get to the dirt later on."

"You've found some dirt?"

"Trust me. I will. There's always dirt in the construction business. Now, can you meet me down at the Vieux Port in half an hour? I have a friend with a boat who can take us out to Frioul. I can get a couple of photographs of Wapping's yacht. Good for the piece."

Sam was smiling as he ended the call. Philippe's enthusiasm was contagious, and he found himself looking forward to the expedition. But first, he wanted to bring Reboul up to date.

When Reboul heard that Patrimonio had been to dinner on the Wapping yacht, his reaction was succinct and unflattering. "The man is *connu pour un parasite*," he said. "A freeloader. He would go to a stranger's funeral if drinks were being served." After hearing about the trip to Frioul, he wished Sam *bon voyage*. "And if you get the chance, drown Wapping."

The Vieux Port was crowded, as it usually was on a sunny morning, and it took Sam several minutes to find Philippe, eventually spotting him in a speedboat tied up alongside one of the island ferries. The ferry captain and a deckhand were leaning over the side flirting with the speedboat's crew, a young blonde dressed for the trip in a yachting cap and what appeared to be a couple of handkerchiefs held together by optimism.

Philippe, looking far from nautical in his black suit, waved to Sam and ushered him on board. "This is my friend Jean-Claude," he said, turning to a small, wiry man, brown as a nut, who was standing by the wheel. "He's the captain, so show some respect. And Birgitta here is his first mate. *Bon. Allons-y!*" And with a burble from the powerful engine as accompaniment, Jean-Claude threaded his way through the neatly moored rows of small sailboats and out into the open sea.

Sam loathed boats. For him, they were cursed with two fundamental disadvantages: there was never enough room, and you couldn't get off. Even so, he found himself enjoying the clean, salty air and the spectacular view of Marseille stretching behind them at the end of their long white wake, as the boat made a gentle southwesterly curve from the Vieux Port.

Jean-Claude explained the route they were taking. "The yacht of Lord Wapping is over there"—he pointed to an island almost straight ahead—"but we cannot see her because she is moored in a bay between the two islands of Ratonneau and Pomègues. These islands block the view from the city. They hide the yacht from anyone looking out from Marseille. It is the most private mooring one could wish for. You will see. Now we go along the north coast of Ratonneau, turn into the Baie du Grand-Soufre, *et voilà.*"

Five minutes later, they entered the bay. Jean-Claude throttled back the engine until they were barely making headway, and there she was, *The Floating Pound* in all her glory, her prow pointing out toward the bay's entrance. Even from a distance she looked enormous, a bone-white colossus, and as they got closer she seemed to swell in size until she threatened to block out most of the sky.

*"Un bon paquet, non?"* said Jean-Claude. "I'll go completely around her so you can see some of the toys."

They went slowly past the imposing bridge, which was flying Lord Wapping's personal pennant, a large *W* bestriding a globe of the world. Then the radar installation, the davits—which Sam noticed were empty at the moment—that would normally hold the yacht's speedboat, the immaculate paintwork and gleaming portholes, and, perched on the stern of the yacht like some enormous, shiny insect, a white helicopter, with large scarlet letters along the side that read *Wapping Air*.

It was while Sam was wondering how many gallons the yacht did to the mile that he realized they were being watched. A young deckhand, dressed in white, was making a thorough study of Birgitta through his binoculars.

"Birgitta?" said Sam. "Do me a favor, will you? Wave to that nice young man on deck."

Birgitta straightened up from her position leaning against the speedboat's windshield, took off her yachting cap and waved it vigorously back and forth, putting the upper part of her swimsuit under severe strain. After a moment's hesitation, the deckhand grinned and waved his binoculars in reply.

Jean-Claude brought the speedboat close enough for conversation.

Sam looked up at the deckhand. "That's a hell of a boat,"
he said. "What a beauty."

Encouraged, no doubt, by the prospect of a close-up view
of Birgitta, the deckhand beckoned them nearer still. "The
owner and the rest of them are all on shore. Do you want to
have a quick look around?"

The deckhand introduced himself as Bob, and he was a man
who had clearly missed his vocation as a tour guide. Describing, explaining, emphasizing, pointing out items of particular
interest, he led the way, with Philippe, who seemed to be having a problem with his cell phone, bringing up the rear. They
were shown the bridge and its navigational marvels, the pad-
ded sunbathing deck and Jacuzzi, the large dining area with
a barbecue big enough for an entire flock of sheep, and the
main salon. Here was a symphony in gold and white—white
walls, gold lamé lampshades, white carpet, gold-framed mirrors, white leather couches and armchairs—prompting Sam
to mutter, "Let's hope nobody gets seasick in here. There's
nowhere to throw up."

The tour ended with a pilgrimage to the helicopter, where
the visitors stood in a respectful arc while Bob recited a few
of the helicopter's vital statistics. Its four-passenger capacity,
its range, its speeds (both cruising and top), the silence of its
engine, the ease of parking, and on and on. Finally, stunned by
this surfeit of information, the visitors were allowed to make
their escape and head back toward port.

Sam, aware that Philippe had been lagging behind the rest

of them, asked him if he had got what he wanted. Philippe held up his phone and grinned. "Enough to fill a photo album."

The wind had freshened, making conversation difficult. Sam watched the waves and let his mind drift back to what he had just seen. As much as he disliked boats, and as much as he found the idea of spending a fortune on one incomprehensible, the visit had caused him to think again about the man he was up against. Despite his suspect tastes in interior decoration, Wapping was without doubt extremely rich. And, as Sam well knew, you don't get that rich by being stupid.

The group sitting at the best table on the terrace of Peron had settled in for a long lunch. If any of them had chosen to look out over the sea at that moment, they might have noticed Jean-Claude's speedboat coming into port, but they were too busy paying attention to their host. Lord William Wapping was holding court.

Seated on his right was a senior member of the development committee, and the main reason for the lunch: Monsieur Faure, a modest-looking man in a quiet gray suit. According to information received from Patrimonio, he was "a little unreliable"—that is, he couldn't be guaranteed to vote as he was told when the time came. It would be helpful, Patrimonio suggested, if Monsieur Faure were to be given a little special attention and made to feel important.

Next to Faure was the only woman in the group, Wapping's companion, Annabel Sykes. The product of a family on the fringes of the aristocracy, her role models—the Duchess of Cornwall and Madonna—were signs of her fascination with both the British establishment and the world of glamour. Vain, good-looking, and infinitely susceptible to bribes in the form of jewelry, designer clothes, silk underwear, and abundant pocket money, she had met Lord Wapping at Ascot, and was literally swept off her feet when he gave her a lift back to town in his helicopter. She was later to describe the moment, with a coy flutter of the eyelashes, as love at first flight.

On her other side was a fellow toff, Tiny de Salis, an Old Etonian gone terribly wrong. He was the skipper of the yacht and pilot of the helicopter. A great barrel of a man (hence his nickname), he enjoyed a discreet rapport with Annabel based on their privileged social origins. Alas, these had not saved de Salis from the results of his addiction to gambling. He had met Lord Wapping, in those days a successful bookmaker, when he had run up debts that he was unable to pay. Indeed, their first meeting had also been attended by Wapping's enforcers, on hand in case it became necessary to encourage payment by breaking one or two arms and legs. De Salis was saved by charm and his abilities with boats and light aircraft, and had ended up paying off his debts by working for his lordship.

Looking even smaller than usual next to the bulk of de Salis was Wapping's personal lawyer, Ray Prendergast, known behind his back as "the Ferret." The size of a jockey and with the instincts of a gangster, he had a reputation, even among his more eminent colleagues in the legal profession, of a man who should not be crossed. There were rumors of his ties to the underworld, of fixing sporting events, suborning witnesses, even of manipulating judges. But nothing had been proved, and he had been highly effective on Lord Wapping's behalf in the matter of tax evasion, property acquisition, stock rigging, and three potentially expensive divorces. (After the most recent of these, he had texted Lord Wapping as follows: "Wife extracted from wallet," a phrase that had subsequently gained some currency among London divorce lawyers.)

The bodyguards, Brian and Dave, glowering at the world through pitch-black sunglasses, completed Wapping's entourage. These two were survivors from the old days, when bookies needed some muscle from time to time, and they found their present life a little tame. As Brian had said to Dave only the other day, they hadn't beaten anyone up for years. Still, the money was good.

Lord Wapping looked down at his empty plate approvingly. These Frogs certainly knew how to cook. He had followed the waiter's advice and ordered the *noisette d'agneau en croûte de tapenade* without being too sure what it was, and had been delightfully surprised by the lamb in a light crust that had been flavored with olives, capers, anchovies, and herbs. Cheese was to come, and then a spot of pudding. And, as they were outside on the terrace, he could finish off with a cigar. Feeling unusually benevolent, he turned to see how his guest of honor, Monsieur Faure, was getting on.

This had been another pleasant surprise. Faure could actually speak English, and had seemed to be receptive to Wapping's tentative first advances. These had included the offer of a trip along the coast on *The Floating Pound,* and perhaps Madame Faure might care to come too. Or perhaps not, Wapping thought, seeing the amount of attention being paid by

Faure to Annabel Sykes. She had chosen to speak to him in her best French—picked up at finishing school in Lausanne—and he was visibly charmed not only by Annabel and her *décolleté* but also by the copious amounts of *rosé* he was getting through.

With Faure happily occupied, Lord Wapping could relax while he considered his next move. Patrimonio was already counting the money he would make from his cut of the construction costs. Faure was looking very cooperative. That left the five other members of the committee, whom Wapping was going to meet at the official cocktail party later on that week. If he could put the fix on two of them, that would constitute a majority. He'd ask Patrimonio to point out a couple of soft targets. He leaned back and beckoned to the wine waiter, and asked for something special to go with the cheese. He deserved it.

Elena closed her eyes and gave in to the deep and soothing pressure, just this side of pain, applied by the fingers of the masseuse as she worked her way down the spine. This had been Mimi's suggestion, as the fitting end to a hectic few hours of sightseeing, shopping, and lunch. She had booked an afternoon of indulgence for them both at the Château Berger spa, high on the Corniche Kennedy. Restorative poultices of warm mud, showers under tiny jets of heated sea water, and forty minutes of reflexology, finishing off with one of the specialties of the house, the *massage énergétique*. Bliss.

The day had begun at a café on the Vieux Port. As is customary with women meeting for the first time, she and Mimi had subjected one another to a thorough, if surreptitious, investigation that included shoes, handbags, sunglasses, hair, and makeup. Each of them had been pleased to see that the other had made an effort—Elena in a sleeveless linen dress of pale lilac, Mimi in narrow black pants and a crisp white jacket.

Over coffee, they had planned their morning, and started it off with one of Marseille's favorite views, the great sweep of city and sea that rewarded those who made the steep climb to Notre-Dame de la Garde. Another good reason for the climb was to see the basilica's remarkable collection of ex-votos, painted by grateful sailors, fishermen, and others who had survived the perils and disasters of the sea. As Mimi said, the images of sinking ships, drowning seamen, storms, and hurricanes did little to encourage a longing for life on the ocean waves, and it was with a renewed fondness for dry land that they made their way down to the relative security of the boutiques in the Rue Paradis and the Rue de Rome.

By now, the two of them were getting on extremely well. In fact, they never stopped talking. Mimi wanted to know all about L.A.—her curiosity having been piqued by Philippe's visit and his subsequent enthusiastic report. Elena was equally interested to hear an insider's rundown of Marseille, Aix, Avignon, and even that distant paradise, Saint-Tropez. The morning passed so pleasantly and so quickly that they were late getting to the restaurant. By the time they arrived, their table—saved because Philippe had been a regular for years—was the only one free.

He had made reservations for them at Le Boucher, in the Rue de Village, a restaurant convincingly disguised as a butcher's shop. At the back of the shop, past the displays of beef, lamb, and veal, a door led to a small, crowded room, shaded from the sun despite its glass roof by the sprawl of a huge bougainvillea. "Philippe thought you'd like this place," said Mimi, "because the meat is so good, and he thinks that red-blooded Americans love their meat." She grinned. "I hope he's right."

"Absolutely." Elena looked around the room, and failed to see anyone resembling a tourist. "I guess they're all French."

Mimi shook her head. "No, no. They're all Marsellais."

Before Elena could pursue this interesting distinction, the waiter came with menus and two flutes of champagne. "Compliments of Monsieur Philippe," he said, "and we have his favorites on the menu today. *En plus*, he has told us to send the bill to him."

Mimi put down her menu and looked at Elena. "Are you feeling hungry?"

Elena thought about her usual working lunch of rabbit food. "Sure. I'm one of those red-blooded Americans."

Mimi nodded at the waiter, who smiled and bustled off to the kitchen.

Elena raised her glass. "Cheers. Do I get to know what we're going to eat?"

"To start, *bresaola* with hearts of artichoke, sun-dried tomatoes, and Parmesan. Then, beef cheeks, with a slice of home-made *foie gras* on top. And a *fondant au chocolat*. Does that sound OK?"

"Sounds like heaven."

The two women made a striking couple, the object of many

an appreciative glance from the mostly male clientele. Elena could perhaps have passed for a local girl, with her black, shoulder-length hair and olive complexion. Mimi, on the other hand, looked as though she were taking the day off from one of the more fashionable streets of Paris. Pale skin, with a light dusting of freckles, and hair—cut almost as short as Philippe's—that was the dark, rich, henna-red that one only sees coming out of a top-class hairdresser. Her face, with its oversized brown eyes and full mouth, was in a constant state of animation, by turns amused, surprised, or fascinated by what Elena had to say. The conversation flowed easily from the usual topics of work, vacations, and clothes before arriving inevitably at a spirited discussion of men (in general) and Sam and Philippe (in particular). These were both judged to be works in progress, capable of further improvement. But promising, promising.

# Seven

Sam was whistling as he strolled back along the garden path that led from the pool to the terrace. He was in a fine, optimistic mood. Today looked set to be another of the three hundred days of sunshine promised each year by the local tourist office. Tonight was Patrimonio's reception, when the job would start to get really interesting. And Elena seemed to have taken to a life of ease with the enthusiasm of a long-term prisoner suddenly given her freedom.

There she was now, sitting at a table on the terrace dressed in a white bathrobe, contemplating a large bowl of *café au lait* and a copy of the *International Herald Tribune*. Sam leaned down to kiss the top of her head, still wet from the shower.

"Good morning, my jewel. How are you today? You should have come for a swim. The water was perfect. I was like a young dolphin."

Elena looked up, squeezing one eye shut against the sun. "I did two lengths of the shower." She reached for her dark glasses. "Tell me something, Sam. What is it that makes you so damn *perky* in the morning?"

Sam poured himself some coffee while he considered his reply. "A clear conscience," he said as he sat down. "And the love of a good woman."

There was a dismissive grunt from Elena. She was never at her best first thing in the morning, whereas Sam was instantly—and irritatingly—lively as soon as he got up. In the past, this had led to some dangerous moments over breakfast. But today, the sun and the surroundings exercised their soothing influence, and the two of them sat in peace over their coffee.

It was Elena who eventually broke the silence. "I forgot to tell you," she said. "Mimi's taken a few days' vacation so she can show me around. Isn't that great? Saint-Tropez, the Luberon, Aix, all over. And today we're doing the boat trip from Cassis to those little creeks along the coast."

"The *calanques*," said Sam. "You can't get to them by road. It's either by boat or on foot. Spectacular spot for a picnic—maybe we'll do that when I'm through with work."

"What's the schedule for today?"

Sam sighed. "Nothing exciting. I have to go to the project office, register, pick up my credentials, smile at everybody, that kind of thing. Then I want to check that the project model has been set up the way it should be. Tonight should be more interesting. That's the reception, when we're all on our best behavior."

"Me too?"

"Especially you. Charming and modest—and no dancing on the tables." Sam finished his coffee, looked at his watch, and got up. "Have fun with Mimi. Don't do anything I wouldn't do."

The project office, overlooking the port in one of the fine old buildings that had been sandblasted, polished, and generally restored to their nineteenth-century glory, seemed to have been staffed by some of the prettiest girls in Marseille. One of them took Sam over to an area that had been screened off, where the project secretary guarded the inner sanctum of the corner office.

Before Sam had finished his first carefully prepared sentence in French, the secretary smiled, held up her hand, and said, "Perhaps it would be better for you in English?"

"I wasn't expecting English."

"We all speak English here. It's part of the Capital of Culture preparations. Even the Marseille taxi drivers are learning English." She smiled again and shrugged. "Or so they say."

She settled Sam into a chair opposite her and asked for identification before passing over a dossier and the forms that had to be filled in. Halfway through the first one, he was distracted by a gust of expensive aftershave as a man walked quickly past him and into the corner office.

"Is he . . . ?"

The secretary nodded. "My boss, Monsieur Patrimonio. He's the chairman of the selection committee."

The sound of a buzzer on the secretary's phone put an end to the conversation, and she was already getting to her feet as she answered. Picking up a notepad, she made her excuses to Sam and hurried through to the office, leaving him to return to his forms. When these had been dealt with, he glanced at the contents of the dossier: a name tag, a thin sheaf of documents, and his handsomely engraved invitation to the reception. He was wondering whether he should leave or stay when the office door opened and the secretary came out, followed by the chairman of the committee and his aftershave.

Patrimonio was a man who took his appearance seriously. His suit was a poem in lightweight pearl-gray worsted, cut in the close-fitting Italian style that leaves precious little room in the pockets for anything more bulky than a silk handkerchief. An extravagant show of sky-blue shirt cuff protruded from the sleeves of his jacket, with a large Panerai watch worn over the left cuff in the manner of Gianni Agnelli. Tall and slim, his hair dark except for wings of gray brushed back from his temples, he was the picture of distinction. Sam felt underdressed in his check shirt and cotton pants.

Patrimonio advanced with hand outstretched. "*Enchanté*, Monsieur Levitt, *enchanté*. Welcome to Marseille. Nathalie told me you were here. I hope she's been looking after you?"

Before Sam had a chance to reply, one of Patrimonio's trouser legs started to vibrate. "Ah. Forgive me," he said, as he slid a paper-thin phone from his pocket before retreating to the privacy of his lair.

"Well," said Sam, "I guess that's the end of our little meeting."

"He's a very busy man." Nathalie smiled, and picked up some papers from her desk. "And now, if you'll excuse me . . ."

Everyone seems to be very busy, thought Sam, except me. He decided to take advantage of his idleness by strolling down to the Vieux Port for a coffee in the sunshine while he went through the official dossier that Nathalie had given him.

He found the sales pitches of the fish-sellers on the Quai des Belges much more entertaining than the documents in the dossier, which had suffered from the dead hand of creation by committee, cliché plodding after cliché in a dreary procession on every page. A brief history of Marseille was followed by a puff for the city's selection as the European Capital of Culture in 2013 (with ten million visitors expected), followed in turn by a heavy-handed description of the charms of the Anse des Pêcheurs, a highly technical account of the process used to select the three finalists, and a reassurance—obligatory in these green times—about the total lack of damage the project would cause to the environment. The whole thing was a classic of its kind, a model of self-important bureaucratic verbiage, and Sam made a mental note to tailor his presentation accordingly. Jokes were out. Gravity would be the order of the day. The very thought of it made him yawn.

Less than three miles away as the seagull flies, Lord Wapping and Ray Prendergast were huddled over a pile of papers in his lordship's private stateroom. They had been going over Wapping's portfolio of business interests, and the news was not good; worse than that, it was potentially disastrous.

The problem was one of excessively optimistic leverage, combined with a couple of what Prendergast described as dodgy downturns in the global economy. Surefire investments had gone sour. Long-shot investments had failed to come off. There were increasingly loud rumblings of discontent from the banks, which were becoming more and more nervous about the huge loans they had made to Wapping. Even the core business of bookmaking was feeling the effects of increased competition, and the money it generated was barely enough to service interest payments.

"In other words, Billy," said Prendergast, "we're stuffed unless this deal goes through. You'll lose your shirt. Mind you, there's still a bit tucked away in the Cayman Islands and Zurich, but you'd have to say goodbye to everything else."

Lord Wapping drew on his cigar as he contemplated a future without the house in Eaton Square, the duplex on Park Avenue, the lodge in Gstaad, the yacht, the racehorses, the stable of overpowered cars. Gone, all of it. And with it, no doubt, Annabel.

Prendergast rubbed his eyes and thought wistfully about a pint of English beer. He was exhausted after spending half the night trying to squeeze some good news out of the figures. He'd also had more than enough of life on board, where he was cramped and fed strange foreign food. As for the French he'd met, he wouldn't give any of them house room. Untrustworthy prima donnas, the lot of them. He'd advised against getting involved with this project right at the start. Ironically, it was now the only chance to save the Wapping empire. "Like

I said, if this doesn't come good, we're stuffed. So what do you reckon the odds are?"

Wapping was a gambling man, and this was the biggest gamble of his life. Millions, many millions, were at stake here, more than enough to settle his debts, with plenty left over for a few new acquisitions. That was his business philosophy, always had been: you have to speculate to accumulate. It had worked well for him in the past, and despite the facts, he remained hopeful about the future. "The trouble with you, my old sunshine, is that you always see the glass half empty instead of half full."

"I spent most of last night looking at the glass, Billy. It's not half empty. It's as dry as a bleeding bone. Not a drop. You don't have to deal with the banks, like I do. Take a look at this lot." Prendergast took a sheaf of papers and fanned them out on the table in front of Wapping—e-mails and letters, all with the same basic message: We want our money, and we want it now.

Naturally, the terminology was a little more subtle. There were "mounting concerns" about the "unacceptable situation." References to the "exceptional fragility" of the market. Regrets that Lord Wapping had been so difficult to contact. And, in every case, there was the urgent wish for Lord Wapping's presence so that matters could be resolved.

"So there you go," said Prendergast. "They're out for blood. Their next step is to call in the law. This is it, Billy. Shit or bust."

Wapping was spared further bad news by the arrival of

Annabel, burnished from a morning spent on the sunbathing deck and dressed for lunch in white jeans and white T-shirt, both one size too tight.

"Sweetie," she said, "I'm just a tiny bit worried about the time." She looked at her watch, one of Cartier's finest. "How long does it take to fly to Monaco? Mustn't be late for lunch—I think one of the royals is going to be there, *très* incognito. One of the Monaco royals, of course, but still."

Ray Prendergast looked up at Annabel, feeling once again a dislike that he'd done his best to conceal since her arrival last year in the Wapping menagerie. A stuck-up bit of posh, he called her privately, out for all she could get, and with ambitions to become the fourth Lady Wapping. In every way, she was an unnecessary expense. And yet Wapping seemed to dote on her. Prendergast tapped the papers in front of him. "Before you go, Billy."

Wapping aimed a shrug of apology at Annabel. "Tell Tiny to warm her up," he said. "I'll be there in a couple of minutes."

Annabel blew him a kiss, scooped up a crocodile handbag the size of a military backpack, and disappeared in the direction of the helicopter.

Wapping glanced down at the papers and ground the remains of his cigar into a crystal ashtray. "Right. E-mail all of them. Tell them I'm deeply involved in final negotiations that will secure a massive construction project in Marseille. These negotiations will be concluded within the next week or two, and I will then return to London to share the good news personally with them." Wapping got to his feet, brushing cigar ash from his shirt front. "There. That should hold the bastards."

"Let's hope so, Billy. Let's hope so."

It is a short, steep walk from the Vieux Port to a magnificent arrangement of buildings known to the Marseillais as La Vieille Charité, or simply La Charité. It was conceived by Pierre Puget, a native of Marseille who became the court architect of Louis XIV, and because of this impeccable architectural pedigree, Patrimonio had chosen it as an appropriate setting for the reception. The evening was to be a kind of premiere—the first time that the three models put forward by Sam and his competitors would be on display, and Sam was anxious to make sure that his model had been correctly installed.

He made his way up through the narrow, twisting streets of the ancient neighborhood known as Le Panier, where Puget had been born in 1620 (by extraordinary coincidence, in a house overlooking the site of the masterpiece he designed nearly fifty years later). As he walked, Sam went back over some of the history of the area he had picked up from conversations with Reboul.

Originally, despite its name, La Charité had been little more than a decorative prison, a place to put the beggars and vagabonds that infested Marseille's streets at the time. Things were so bad that the city was known as a gigantic *cour des miracles,* an ironic term, to say the least, for a slum, and the merchants of Marseille decided that they could no longer tolerate it. Criminal elements, after all, were bad for business. And so they were rounded up, shut away, and only allowed out to work as forced labor. So much for charity.

Things got a little better after the Revolution. The elderly and infirm, the destitute and homeless were taken in, but not forced to work. And so La Charité staggered along until it was closed at the end of the nineteenth century. After one final spasm of activity during the 1914–1918 war, when it was turned into a base for a corps of nurses, it was left to rot.

It wasn't until the 1960s that Marseille decided to do something about one of its architectural treasures, and after twenty years of painstaking restoration work, La Charité had once again become something that Pierre Puget could be proud of.

Sam hadn't known quite what to expect. Reboul's description had been so extravagant, with so many pauses for fingertips to be kissed, that Sam had prepared himself for a disappointment, or at least a slight letdown. But as he was passing through the double iron gates that guarded the entrance he was stopped in his tracks, stunned by the extraordinary sight in front of him. It was an immense quadrangle, built around a courtyard perhaps a hundred yards long and fifty yards wide. Surrounding the courtyard was a series of three-story buildings, their façades pierced by an elegant succession of arches leading to an interior gallery that ran the entire distance of the ground floor. And in the middle of the courtyard stood a charming domed chapel. Time had softened all the stone to a color somewhere between faded pink and cream, and in the morning sun the entire courtyard glowed.

Some years before, La Charité had taken on a new role as

a home for museums of art and archaeology. Inside the chapel was a permanent sculpture exhibition, and it was here that Patrimonio had arranged to hold the reception. Sam passed through a quartet of massive columns and into the entrance to the chapel, where he was immediately confronted by a large woman holding a clipboard.

*"On est fermé, Monsieur."* The words were uttered—and the inevitable stern finger wagged—with barely disguised satisfaction, as is often the case when French petty authority tells you that what you want to do is impossible. Sam gave her his best smile and showed her his invitation, his dossier, and even his name tag, all of which she peered at with considerable suspicion before standing aside to let him in.

Inside the chapel, groups of people armed with crates of bottles and glasses hurried to and fro putting the finishing touches to a bar that had been set up in an alcove under the blind stare of a marble statue. Taking up much of the far end of the chapel were three long tables, each draped in a white cloth. The project models, one per table, had been arranged so that the lowest, Reboul's apartment block, was in the middle, towered over by the skyscrapers on either side. Models were identified by the names of their backers: Wapping Enterprises, London; Van Buren & Partners, New York; and Eiffel International, Paris.

As far as Sam could see, the installations had been done carefully and correctly. He was bracing himself for another encounter on his way out with the dragon at the door—no doubt to include a strip search in case he'd decided to steal one of the smaller sculptures—when he found he had company.

A slim, dark-haired woman in a black pantsuit had arrived, apparently also to inspect the models. She was attractive in that slightly vulpine way brought about by years of strict dieting, and, as Sam quickly noticed, immaculately made up. Late thirties, by the look of her, but who could tell for sure with French women?

"Hi. See anything you like?"

The woman turned to face Sam, her eyebrows raised, her blue eyes glacial. "And you are?"

"Sam Levitt." He nodded toward his model. "I'm with Van Buren." He extended his hand, and the woman extended hers, palm down, leaving Sam of three minds as to whether to shake it, kiss it, or admire the manicure.

"Caroline Dumas. I represent Eiffel. So we are competitors."

"Looks like it," said Sam. "What a pity."

Madame Dumas inclined her head and attempted a smile. Sam did the same. She turned away from him to resume her inspection of the models.

Back outside in the sunlit quadrangle, Sam wondered if French women took lessons in the art of the brush-off, or if it was something instinctive, implanted at birth. He shook his head, and went off in search of lunch.

# Eight

It was cocktail hour at La Charité, and a line of guests stretched from the door of the chapel to halfway across the courtyard. The line had formed because Patrimonio, relishing his role as the gracious host, had decided to follow the example of royalty and heads of state and greet each of his guests personally. And so they waited in the evening sunlight with varying degrees of impatience, entertained by a string quartet that was playing Mozart in the long gallery.

Elena and Sam joined the end of the line, taking a look at their fellow guests as they went. They were mostly Marseille businessmen and their wives, suntanned and jolly, a tribute to the invigorating qualities of pastis. There were also some visiting bureaucrats, with their pallid northern complexions, a three-man team from the local television station, one or two smartly dressed couples—presumably friends of Patrimonio—and a press photographer. There was no sign of Philippe, who had arrived early to take a good look at the models.

Sam noticed Caroline Dumas, chic in dark-gray silk, talking on her cell phone. They made eye contact. Sam nodded. Madame Dumas raised her eyebrows. "Somehow I don't think she's a fan of yours," said Elena. "Who is she?"

"Madame Dumas, one of the competition. From Paris. See if you can pick out the one from England, Lord Wapping."

"What does he look like?"

"English, I guess. Bulletproof pinstripe suit, big tie, good shoes, bad teeth—wait a minute. I think that must be him. Over there, with the blonde."

Sam's guess was confirmed by the sound of a guffaw and a loud English voice. "Well, he asked for it, didn't he? What a prat." The speaker shook his head and looked at his watch. "If Jérôme doesn't get his finger out we'll be here all night."

He was with Annabel, in what she called her LBD, or little black dress, and another couple. The man could have been Wapping's younger brother—like him, short, florid, and burly. Both men were wearing well-cut suits that almost disguised their bulk. The fourth member of the group, taller than the rest of them by a good five or six inches, was an Amazonian girl of exceptional beauty, most of which was on display thanks to a silver dress of exceptional brevity.

"She doesn't look English," said Sam.

Elena sniffed. "She doesn't look real."

The line gave a sudden lurch forward, and it was only a few minutes before they were being greeted by their host. Patrimonio had changed for the occasion, and had chosen a putty-colored linen suit, set off by the jaunty red and gold striped tie usually reserved for members of London's Marylebone Cricket Club. Sam had the impression that there had been another generous application of aftershave since that morning.

"Monsieur Levitt, I believe. How delightful. And who is this?" He took Elena's hand as though he had no intention of giving it back, and without waiting for Sam's reply, bent over to kiss it.

"Elena Morales," said Sam. "This is her first visit to Provence."

"Ah, mademoiselle. Make me a happy man. Stay forever." Patrimonio, exuding gallantry, at last released her hand. Elena smiled at him. He straightened his tie and smoothed his hair.

"Well, you were certainly a hit," said Sam, as they moved into the chapel and toward the bar. "I thought he was going to ask you to dance."

Elena shook her head. "I can't get too excited about guys who wear more perfume than I do. But the hand-kissing I could get used to."

"I'll practice." He signaled to the bartender. "What are you having?"

"Daddy told me I should never say no to champagne." Elena looked around at the chapel—the alcoves around the side, each with its graceful arch and marble statue, the lovely proportions of the room, the domed ceiling, the soft evening light filtering through the high windows—and let out a sigh. "This is magic. Why don't we do buildings like this anymore?"

Armed with their champagne, they began to do their duty

and mingle. Sam found Patrimonio's secretary and asked her to introduce them to members of the committee, who were standing in a pensive group in front of the three project models. The introductions were made, Elena was discreetly admired by the committee, and Sam answered the not-too-searching questions put to him by Monsieur Faure, who seemed to be the senior member. Sam was distracted for a moment by the sight of Philippe coming through the crowd glued to his cell phone. As agreed, they didn't acknowledge one another.

Monsieur Faure nodded toward the bar. "Have you met your competitor Lord Wapping? A most sociable man. Let me introduce you."

Sam's first impression of Wapping had surprised him. He had expected a conventional product of Wall Street and the City: serious, quietly arrogant as rich men tend to be, and dull. Instead, he found himself looking at a plump, jovial face that would have been benign except for the shrewd and calculating eyes that were now focused on Sam with unblinking intensity.

"So you're the Yank who wants to put up a block of flats," Wapping said with a grin .

"That's me," said Sam. "This is Elena Morales." He pointed toward the row of models. "And there's my block of flats."

"Well, good luck, mate. May the best man win, as long as it's me." He clapped Sam on the shoulder. "Just kidding. Here, meet Annabel."

As Annabel looked at Sam, her eyes widened—an old *femme fatale* trick—as though she had never seen such an attractive man in her life. "You must have been told this a thousand times," she said, "but I can't resist. You look just like a blond George Clooney."

Elena suppressed a snort as she nodded to Annabel.

Wapping continued with the introductions. "This layabout is Mikey Simmons. Nothing to do with the project. He's in top-end motors. Exclusive concession in Saudi and Dubai. Astons, Ferraris, Rollers, whatever you want. And here"—Wapping turned toward the statuesque young lady—"here we have Raisa from Moscow." Feeling that he had discharged his social responsibilities, Wapping looked at his glass, found it empty, and waved it at the bartender. "Oy, Jean-Claude! I could murder another glass of champagne."

Sam made their excuses and steered Elena away from the bar. "Now you've seen the competition, what do you think?"

"I can see why Lord Wapping gets his own way. He's like a human bulldozer. As for the blonde, she's a real piece of work."

"Is that a compliment?"

"No."

They had stopped at the edge of the crowd when Sam's eye was caught by a couple sharing an alcove with one of the statues: Patrimonio was chatting to Caroline Dumas, and Sam was not surprised to see that she was a great deal more lively and friendly with Patrimonio than she had been with him. She gazed up at him when he spoke, she rested her hand on his arm when she replied, she showed all the signs of a woman fascinated by what her companion had to say. Patrimonio, naturally, was enjoying this display of attention from a pretty Parisienne, and it was with obvious irritation that he had to break off their conversation when it was interrupted by the arrival of a third person.

It was Philippe. Even from a distance, Elena and Sam could see that the encounter was not amicable. Philippe was waving an accusing finger in Patrimonio's face. Patrimonio was swatting it away. And Caroline Dumas, lips pursed in disapproval, had tactfully stepped aside to commune with the statue. The scene had the makings of a brawl. And then Philippe abruptly turned on his heel and stalked out of the chapel, leaving Patrimonio to smooth his hair and calm himself in preparation for his big moment: the speech.

Sam noticed that the string quartet had filed in from the gallery. He was wondering if the speech was to be delivered with a musical accompaniment when Patrimonio's secretary asked him to go and stand next to Lord Wapping and Caroline Dumas in front of their respective models. There they waited while Patrimonio fiddled with his notes and cleared his throat. He nodded to his secretary. She tapped loudly on the rim of her glass with her silver pen. The chapel fell silent.

Patrimonio started quietly enough by thanking his audience for coming to what he referred to as a very important evening; indeed, a landmark in the history of the great city of Marseille. Sam glanced to one side and saw that Wapping, still clinging to his champagne glass, was wearing an expression of glazed incomprehension. He clearly didn't understand a word of what was being said in such carefully enunciated French.

It wasn't long before Patrimonio became more animated as he described the talent, the hard work, the *vision* of his committee. And perhaps, he added with due modesty, as chairman of this galaxy of stars he too had played his part. Moving on to the projects that had been proposed, Patrimonio introduced Caroline Dumas, Wapping, and Sam to the audience, leading a round of applause for each one. The models were there to be inspected, he said, and he was sure that the ideas they represented were of such excellence that choosing one of them would be most difficult. However, he was confident that the members of the committee were up to the task. They had done their homework, and they hoped to have reached a decision within the next two weeks. Finally, with a flourish worthy of a great conductor, he stretched out both arms to the string quartet, which broke into a spirited rendering of "La Marseillaise."

As the last notes died away Sam rejoined Elena, who had been standing not far from Wapping's friends. She had heard him confess to them that the only parts of the speech that were familiar to him were his name, and that tune of theirs at the end—"the whatsit, you know, the Mayonnaise."

None of the French showed any signs of going as long as the champagne kept flowing, and so Sam and Elena were able to slip away unnoticed. They were crossing the quadrangle when Sam's phone rang. It was Philippe.

"I had a little *contretemps* with Patrimonio."

"We saw. What was it all about? Where are you?"

"Just around the corner. There's a bar called Le Ballon, in the Rue du Petit-Puits. You can almost see it from La Charité. I'll be waiting outside, OK?"

On his previous visit to Marseille, Sam had experienced Philippe's fondness for disreputable bars, and this was another scruffy example. Above the door, a tin sign that had seen better days had been decorated with a painting of a soccer ball, *le ballon,* next to a small wine glass, also known as *un ballon,* brimming with a lurid mixture that the artist hoped could be mistaken for red wine. Philippe, neat and well pressed in his black suit and white shirt, looked very much out of place.

They pushed through the bead curtain at the entrance, to be greeted by a sudden silence and the stares of half a dozen men who looked up for a moment before returning to their newspapers and dominoes. The national ban on smoking in enclosed public spaces was being enthusiastically ignored, and a rising tide of nicotine had long ago obscured the original paintwork. But the room was clean, and not without a certain battered charm. Plain wooden chairs and marble-topped tables bearing the scars of the years were arranged along two of the walls, a third wall was taken up by a long table that had been laid for a meal, and the fourth by a bar and a very elderly bartender. In a far corner, a stout swinging door suggested the presence of a kitchen.

Apart from a flat-screen television above the dining table with the sound turned off, the decorations were limited to large framed photographs, some faded with age, of the Olympique de Marseille soccer teams over the years. "The owner of this place, Serge, used to play for the OM," said Philippe, "until his leg was broken by some *salaud* in a game against Paris Saint-Germain. That's his father behind the bar. Now, what are you going to have?"

They settled for a carafe of *rosé "supérieur,"* which Philippe fetched from the bar, and then Elena and Sam sat back to listen to his account of the exchange with Patrimonio.

Philippe was hoping for an interview, but it had started badly when Patrimonio had introduced him to Caroline Dumas as "the local hack." Philippe grimaced at the memory. "He was showing off in front of her, obviously. And I know I shouldn't care what that pompous old fart says. But he was so condescending it got under my skin. And it got worse. When I asked him a couple of questions, he looked down his nose at me. 'Don't bother me now,' he said. 'Call my secretary if you want to arrange an interview.' This was a public event, for God's sake. He was presenting the projects, and he wouldn't talk to the press? That really annoyed me, and that was when I said something I guess I shouldn't have." He paused to take a swig of wine. "I asked him if he thought it was ethical behavior to accept the hospitality of one of the competitors. He said he didn't know what I was talking about, and so I suggested that we go over and get Lord Wapping's confirmation. Then it started to get ugly, and I left."

"How much of this did Caroline Dumas hear?"

"Only the beginning. After that, she made herself scarce." Philippe drained his glass, and refilled it from the carafe. "But there was one bright spot in the evening. I spoke to all the committee members, and most of them seem to like your idea—one of them actually said he'd be interested in an apartment." The bar had been filling up while Philippe had been talking, with the new arrivals taking up their places at the long table against the wall. A young girl came out of the kitchen at the back and started taking orders for drinks. The old man remained behind the bar. Table service was obviously not included in his professional duties.

"Is this Tuesday?" Philippe consulted his watch. "I thought so. Once a week Serge's wife does tripe, and tonight must be tripe night. The Provençal version is called *pieds et paquets*—feet and parcels. Serge's wife makes the best in Marseille. Are you feeling hungry?"

Elena looked at Sam, and shrugged. "I've never had tripe. What is it exactly?"

"Basically," said Philippe, "it's a mixture of sheep's intestines. Some butchers call it organ meat. In this recipe, the tripe is cut into small squares and made into *paquets* stuffed with lean bacon, parsley, garlic, onions, carrots, olive oil, white wine, chopped tomatoes, and—very important—sheep's feet. It needs to be gently simmered for several hours, of course."

"Of course," said Sam. "You wouldn't want a half-cooked sheep's foot." He turned to Elena. "What do you think? Sounds interesting. You want to try it?"

Elena had been listening to Philippe with mounting horror. "You know what? I had a big lunch. I think I'll pass."

# Nine

"BÉTON SUR MER!" screamed the headline in *La Provence*: concrete by the sea. This was followed by several hundred words, none of them complimentary, about what was referred to as the creeping menace of high-rise buildings along the Marseille coastline.

Philippe had perhaps overdone it, partly as a result of his squabble with Patrimonio. He had begun by reminding his readers about two or three well-known local eyesores that had been built since the fifties. Time and sloppy upkeep had turned them into sad, stained concrete hulks, which Philippe had described as scabs on the face of Marseille. Is this, he asked rhetorically, what the inhabitants of a great city would choose to live with? Do they want more of the same?

It was not only concrete that offended Philippe. It was the size, and above all the height, of these massive slabs that he claimed were destroying the Marseille skyline. How long would it be before the golden statue of the Virgin Mary that crowns the basilica of Notre-Dame de la Garde was obscured by an office high-rise? Or the old buildings around the Vieux Port replaced by multistory garages and hotels? At what point would the people of Marseille say enough!

This brought Philippe to the crux of his article: the dangers and opportunities of building on the Anse des Pêcheurs. It was a choice, he argued, between high-rise and low-rise, between a building designed to extract money from tourists and a building designed to provide homes for locals. He was careful not to mention any names; but then, he didn't have to. It was very clear where his sympathies lay.

As one might expect, Philippe's article received mixed reviews. A jovial Reboul called Sam to congratulate him on planting a useful piece of propaganda, and refused to believe it when Sam said he had had nothing to do with it.

Patrimonio was furious, and immediately called the newspaper's editor to demand a front-page retraction. In reply, he received a brisk lecture on that most precious commodity, journalistic integrity. To further spoil his day, there was a call from an icy Caroline Dumas expressing her profound displeasure.

Lord Wapping, once the article had been translated for him, was seething with anger. He summoned Ray Prendergast for a council of war.

"Ray," he said, chewing on his cigar with irritation, "this is unacceptable. Totally unacceptable." He shoved the newspaper away with the back of his hand. "What can we do about this little tosser?"

Prendergast didn't need to think for long. "Same as we always do, Billy. Offer him cash or a couple of broken legs. Never fails. Do you want me to have a word with the lads?"

Wapping considered the respective merits of bribery and violence. There was no doubt that a session with Brian and Dave would curb the journalist's enthusiasm for the story. On the other hand, if he could be bought, there was a good chance that he could be persuaded to put the case for Wapping's project in another article—or indeed in a series of articles. Cash, he decided.

"But let's keep it in the family, Ray. I'd like you to do the necessary."

"Suppose he doesn't speak English?"

"He'll speak English when he sees the money. You can count on it."

The meeting was about to break up when Wapping's phone rang, with an agitated Patrimonio on the other end. Wapping cut him short.

"No need to get your knickers in a twist, Jérôme. We're dealing with it. No, don't ask. You don't want to know."

A relieved but slightly puzzled Patrimonio put his phone down and pressed the buzzer on his desk. His secretary appeared. "Nathalie," he said, "you have very good English. What is this knickers in a twist?"

Sam took a second and more careful look at the article before calling Philippe.

"Well, my friend," he said, "I think you might have made

one or two enemies this morning. Have you had any reactions yet?"

"My editor likes it. Patrimonio doesn't. Mimi thinks it's great. We'll start getting reactions from readers later today. What did you think of it?"

"Wouldn't want to change a word. But I guess you won't be getting too many fan letters from Wapping and Caroline Dumas."

Philippe laughed. "If I wanted to be popular I'd have been a politician. What are you doing today?"

"Working on my presentation. And I have a few calls to make. How about you?"

"You won't believe this. There's a demonstration this afternoon on one of the beaches by the local branch of Nudistes de France. They want the law changed so they can sunbathe naked. Should be fun."

Sam wondered how someone like Philippe would go down in California.

He got back to his presentation. It was nearly there, except for one crucial decision. Where should it take place? Sam had an idea, but it was complicated, and he couldn't organize it by himself. He got back on the phone, this time to Reboul.

"Francis, I think it's time we got together. I want you to look at the presentation, and I have a couple of ideas I'd like to bounce off you. Do you have any time later on today?"

There was a rustle of paper as Reboul looked through his diary. "I could make myself free between four and six this afternoon. But Sam, we must be careful not to be seen together. Marseille is full of nosy people with big mouths." Reboul was silent for a moment, and then Sam heard him chuckle. "Of course. I know just the place. I have a little ranch in the Camargue. It is perfectly private. Olivier can drive you there. Shall we say 4:30?"

The only two things Sam knew about the Camargue were that it was flat and that it was inhabited for part of the year by flamingos along with a particularly large and ferocious member of the mosquito family. While he waited on the terrace for Olivier he glanced through a guidebook he'd picked up from the house library and was immediately intrigued.

The Camargue had supplied some of the first cowboys in America—men who had left the flamingos for a new life in the bayous of Louisiana and East Texas. Those who had stayed behind became known as *gardians*. They looked after the native black longhorn cattle which, unlike normal cattle, could not only survive but flourish on the Camargue's salt grass. For transport, the *gardians* used another native of the Camargue—the elegant descendants of the white horse introduced by the Arabs many centuries before.

Today, the guide continued, the Camargue is probably best known for its salt, and is sometimes described as the salt cellar of France. And it is no ordinary salt. The *fleur de sel*—the jewel of the salt pans, still gathered in the traditional way by man and his wooden shovel—is regarded as a supreme delicacy. Sam had always thought of salt as little more than white dust, and he shook his head as he read on, the prose waxing more and more ecstatic about the effects of *fleur de sel* applied to a raw radish. Only in France.

The big car came to a stop below the terrace, and Sam

settled into the passenger seat for the journey to Arles and then down into the Camargue. Olivier, delighted to practice his English on a captive audience, explained how Reboul had come to be the owner of a ranch.

It had started off pleasantly enough when Reboul had invited a few acquaintances over for a poker game. Luck was running for Reboul that night, and he was collecting his winnings at the end of the evening when one of the others, a Marseille property dealer named Leconte, announced that he wasn't ready to stop. He had lost consistently during the evening, and had consoled himself a little too generously with Reboul's single malt Scotch. He also suffered from the conviction that he was a better poker player than Reboul, and wanted to prove it. Leconte had always been inclined to arrogance and boastfulness, and whisky made him worse. He proposed a two-handed game, just him and Reboul, for what he called serious stakes—not the small change they had been playing for so far.

Reboul tried to persuade Leconte to drop the idea: it was late, and they all had to work the next day. But Leconte made the great mistake of inferring that Reboul was scared to play for big stakes, and persisted in his demand to keep playing, so Reboul humored him and let Leconte propose the stakes. Each player put up one euro. If Leconte won, he could buy Reboul's yacht for his euro; if Reboul won, he could buy Leconte's property in the Camargue for the same price.

"I was there, serving the drinks," said Olivier. "It was very *dramatique*, like a movie. And when Monsieur Reboul won, he tried to make a joke of it, and gave Leconte back his euro to cancel the debt. But Leconte refused. It was a matter of honor, he said. *Et voilà.*"

"Where is Leconte now?"

"Oh, he said Marseille was becoming too provincial for him. He sold his business and moved to Morocco."

By now, they had left the autoroute linking Marseille and Arles and had turned south on one of the minor roads leading down to the coast. The landscape had changed; it was flat, vast, and empty. The sky, with no silhouettes of buildings, trees, or hills to interrupt it, seemed suddenly bigger. If the sun hadn't been shining, Sam thought, it would all seem quite sinister.

"Does Monsieur Reboul come here often?"

"Once or twice in the spring. Sometimes at Christmas—and usually when one of the mares has little ones. He loves to see his horses when they're babies."

The road was getting narrower, the surface cracked and crumbling. It seemed to be leading directly into the depths of the Camargue swamp when the car swung sharply to the right, past a wooden sign marked PRIVÉ, and down a graveled track. On they drove for perhaps half a mile before they came to a post-and-rail paddock with a range of stabling at one end. A dozen handsome horses, all of them white, gave the car a cursory glance and a flick of the tail as it passed. Another hundred yards and they had reached the ranch.

It was an example of the haphazard school of architecture—a low, sprawling, *L*-shaped building made principally of wood, with windows of assorted sizes and a covered veranda running along the southern side. Three dogs interrupted their siestas to come over and sniff the car before returning to loll on the veranda. When Olivier turned off the engine, the silence was almost overwhelming. Sam got out and stretched as he looked around. He could imagine that nothing much had changed in the past hundred years. The only concession to the twenty-first century was the helicopter parked behind the house.

"Monsieur Reboul must be here already," said Olivier. "That's what he calls his Camargue taxi."

They were halfway toward the massive front door when it opened and a small figure came out to greet them. He was dressed in black trousers, a black waistcoat, and a white shirt, with a face the color of old mahogany, and slightly bandy legs. Olivier introduced him as Luc.

"He lives on the property as a guardian, and he's a genius with horses." Olivier turned to Luc and clapped him on the shoulder. *"Les chevaux sont vos enfants, eh?"*

The little man nodded and smiled, adding yet more wrinkles to a face already pickled and rutted by the sun. He raised a hand to his ear, thumb and little finger extended. *"Monsieur Francis parle sur son portable. Venez!"* He led the way into the house and what was obviously the main room, dominated by an enormous fireplace. Lining the walls were paintings and black-and-white photographs of horses and flamingos, and overflowing bookshelves. The horns of a huge black bull's head served as a hat rack. The furniture was wood and rough leather, primitive but comfortable.

Reboul finished his call and beckoned Sam over. "My dear Sam, welcome to the Camargue. What can I offer you?

Coffee? A beer? Something stronger to keep the mosquitoes away? Come and sit down."

The two men settled in front of a window overlooking the long, flat view. "Interesting place you've got here," said Sam. "Do you have much land?"

Reboul shook his head. "Not a lot—about a hundred acres. We grow a little rice, but the land is mainly for the horses, and it keeps Luc happy. You know, his father was one of the old-style *gardians*, and he taught Luc to ride when he was four. By the time he was ten, he was working." Reboul took a look at his watch. "Now then. We'd better start."

Sam took a sheaf of papers from a folder and passed them over to Reboul. "There's some helicopter reading for you. It's the script. Perhaps you could take a look at it as soon as you can and see if there's anything you think should be changed. I'm told that the committee speaks English, but to be safe I want to have this translated into French and put in a document that we can give to each of the members to take away. My friend Philippe can help me with that."

Reboul gave a nod of approval. "Good idea. Perhaps with a photograph of the project model? Or an artist's impression? What do you think?"

It was Sam's turn to nod. "An artist's impression would be best. It would allow us to cheat a bit, and put in some background touches." He scribbled a note on his folder. "Right. Now we come to the big decision." He reached for his beer and took a long swallow. "Where should we hold the presentation? The chapel of La Charité has already been used. A standard office in a standard office building or a conference room in a big hotel won't work; they're exactly what we're competing against. Also, they're anonymous and boring, and what I'd like to do is to give the committee something different, something that they won't forget in a hurry. I'd like to do it on the beach."

Reboul's eyebrows shot up, and then he smiled. "Of course. Let me guess. The Anse des Pêcheurs?"

"Exactly. It's perfect. I want to get a tent—a big tent, a marquee—put up. We'll make it into a kind of informal conference room, with a long table and chairs for the committee, maybe a bar—"

"Definitely a bar."

". . . and we'll make the presentation at the end of the working day, in the early evening, just as the sun's beginning to go down. I've been down there to check out the sunset. It's spectacular." Sam paused, and waited for Reboul's reaction.

Reboul shook his head. "Sam, what can I say except bravo? As you say, it's perfect, a real *coup de théâtre*. But you're going to need help, and it can't be seen to come from me." He stared out of the window, then nodded to himself before turning back to Sam. "Luckily, I have one or two contacts. I will ask one of them to call you. His name is Gaston. You can trust him. He is extremely discreet. And if anybody should ask how you came to know him, you simply say you met him at a cocktail party." Reboul stood up, came across to Sam, and administered the ultimate seal of approval, a kiss on each cheek. "Congratulations, my friend. Congratulations."

# Ten

"Sam, I think I have a problem." Philippe's voice sounded concerned and slightly breathless. "It's business. Can we talk?"

By now, Sam was familiar enough with Philippe's working methods to know that one could never conduct an important conversation with him over the phone; it had to be face to face. And with Philippe, there was always a little bar somewhere. "Sure. Where do you want to meet?"

"There's a little bar in the Rue de Bir-Hakeim, near the fish market. Le Cinq à Sept. In half an hour. Is that OK?"

True to form, Le Cinq à Sept was as Sam had come to expect from Philippe's bars—small and seedy, with the inevitable photograph, in a place of honor behind the bar, of last year's Marseille soccer team. A scattering of old men, saving up their stubble for the weekly shave, seemed to be the only other customers. Philippe was half hidden in a dim corner. He raised a hand in greeting. "Thanks for coming. I ordered you a pastis—it's safer here than the wine."

Sam topped up his glass with water as Philippe started to talk.

"An hour or so ago, I was leaving the office when this guy stepped in front of me—a little runt in a sharp suit—and asked me in English if I was Mister Davin. When I told him I was, he said this could be my lucky day. Well, you never know where the next tip-off is going to come from, so I agreed to go with him to a café to hear what he had to say. I'm not sure what I was expecting: some story about the English and their yachts, I thought. They often get into trouble down here. Anyway, he started off by telling me he'd seen the piece I did on the Anse des Pêcheurs development, and it had really offended his client."

"Did he say who his client was?"

"He didn't need to. After a couple of minutes it was obvious that he was working for the Englishman Wapping."

"How did he recognize you?"

"It's the haircut. Remember? There's a head shot of me at the beginning of the piece. Well, I gave him the usual stuff about the freedom of opinion in the press, and that my editor would probably be happy to give equivalent space in the paper to another point of view. He looked quite pleased with that, nodding and smiling, and then he took out an envelope. A fat envelope." Philippe paused to take a drink.

" 'Exactly,' this little *con* said, 'another point of view. And you're just the man to write it. Perhaps you might like some encouragement.' Then he slid the envelope over to me. 'You'll find ten thousand euros in there,' he said, 'and there's more where that came from. A nice little earner, and it's all yours for a couple of favorable pieces. This is just between you and me, you understand. Nobody else needs to know.' "

"Suppose you went to the police?" said Sam.

Philippe shook his head. "And tell them what—someone tried to give me ten thousand euros? They'd tell me to get lost."

"So what did you do?"

"I told him I didn't take bribes. Grow up, he said. This is France—everyone takes bribes. That was when I lost it. I told him to take his envelope and shove it up his ass. I said that in French, so he probably didn't understand it, but he would have understood the tone of my voice. And then I left. What do you think I should do?"

"What else can you do? If you don't have any witnesses, it's your word against his. And if he works for Wapping, you can be sure there's a crooked lawyer around somewhere who'd swear that the meeting never happened." Sam shook his head. "No. Try to forget about it. I don't think he'll risk coming back, in case you're ready for him with a recorder in your pocket. Now, I've got something that might cheer you up: a little scoop. I've got to work out the details, but here's the idea."


Ray Prendergast, his mission unaccomplished, fiddled nervously with the envelope on the desk in front of him while he waited for Lord Wapping to get off the phone. His lordship didn't take kindly to failure.

The call over, Wapping poked at the envelope with a thick index finger. "So he didn't bite?"

"Afraid not, Billy."

"What did he say?"

"Well, the last bit was in French, so I didn't get all of it. But basically, he told me to piss off."

"Silly boy. Very silly boy." Wapping sighed, as if he'd been disappointed by the foolish behavior of a close friend. "Doesn't leave us much option, does he? You'd better talk to Brian and Dave. Tell them to teach him a lesson. But Ray?" Wapping lowered his voice. "Nothing terminal. Know what I mean? We don't want any complications. Tell the lads to make it look like an accident."

There are certain men, blessed from birth, whose character and appearance inspire instant liking. Gaston Poirier was such a man: an oversized cherub with a pear-shaped body, a chubby, red-cheeked face, and a mop of curly gray hair. His brown eyes twinkled, and his mouth seemed to be permanently on the brink of a grin. Reboul had said he was the best fixer in Marseille. Sam had warmed to him at first sight.

They were sitting on the terrace, a bottle of *rosé* between them. "I haven't been back to this house since Francis lived here," said Gaston. "There were some parties then, I can tell you—girls, champagne, more girls. Wonderful times." He raised his glass. "Here's to his new project. Tell me all about it."

As Sam went through the background, Gaston made serious inroads on the *rosé,* dabbing his forehead between glasses with a silk handkerchief as though he found the effort of drinking to be truly thirsty work. But he proved to be a model listener, silent and attentive, and when Sam had finished, he nodded several times, an indication that he liked what he had heard.

"The tent is a good idea," he said. "Now we must make it work. For the tent itself, *pas de soucis,* no problem. But the beach is uneven, so you will need a level, solid plank floor. Also electricity. We might need a generator, but I know a guy, an artist with anything electrical, who can tap us into the city's power grid. And then a projector, a conference table and chairs, and maybe"—here Gaston paused to waggle his eyebrows—"a nice little bar with, *bien sûr,* a nice little barmaid. Have I forgotten anything?"

Sam knew France well enough to be extremely wary of the long arm of bureaucracy. Someone, somewhere in the city's administrative labyrinth would have to be consulted, flattered, massaged, possibly taken out to lunch. "There is one thing," he said. "I'm sure we'll need a permit."

"Oh, that." Gaston waved a dismissive hand. "*Pas de soucis.* The mayor is an intelligent man. He will realize that this will be good for Marseille's image as a *dynamique* city, getting ready for 2013." Gaston winked, and tapped the side of his nose. "Besides, we go hunting together in the winter. We're friends. Maybe you should invite him to the presentation. Anyway, I think I can promise you that we won't have any trouble with permits. When do you want to do it?"

• • •

The next two days passed slowly for Brian and Dave, but with a pleasant undercurrent of anticipation. It had been a long time since they had been given a chance to do what they did best, which was to inflict grievous bodily harm — or, as they would describe it, putting the boot in. And as a bonus, the victim was French. Like many Englishmen of their class and generation, they were ardent chauvinists. Here was an opportunity to strike a blow for Mother England against the teeming masses of foreigners who were taking over the world, including most of England's best soccer clubs.

They were sitting in a bar on the Vieux Port, which they had chosen because it called itself a pub, a description that, for them, held out the promise of warm beer, darts, and a large TV set permanently tuned to a snooker tournament. Unfortunately, it was a pub in name only, without even a dart board. The television was tuned to a game show, with a lot of Frogs shouting the odds, and the beer was chilled. But it would have taken more than these shortcomings to blunt their enthusiasm for the task in hand.

So far, they had spent much of the past two days shadowing Philippe and learning his routine. They had followed him in their rented van as he commuted by scooter between the offices of *La Provence* on the Avenue Roger Salengro and his apartment in an old building just off the Corniche, the broad road that follows the coastline. Dave found it close to ideal, an excellent spot to stage an accident. Plenty of room to maneuver, he thought, and then there was that nasty old drop from the road to the rocks below. Landing on them would slow a man down.

"Tell you what, Bri," said Dave. "It looks like a bike job to me—one in front of him, one behind. Crash helmets, so nobody can clock our faces. No worries." Brian nodded sagely. He always left organizational details to Dave, content to limit his own role to the more physical side of their assignments. This time, however, there was one detail that even he could see might be a problem.

"But we haven't got any bikes."

"We nick 'em, Bri. We nick 'em. You have a look when we get back out on the street. There's bikes parked all over the place. Some of them even have a helmet hanging off the handlebars. Or else the helmet will be in that box behind the saddle, and my old mum could open one of those with a nail file."

Brian nodded again. This was what he liked about working with Dave: his grasp of the fine points. By now, Brian's beer had become warm enough to drink. As he took a cautious swallow, he thought longingly of something tasty to go with the beer—a proper English pork pie, the kind served in his favorite pub, The Mother's Ruin, in Stepney. Of course, the Frogs didn't understand about these things. All the rubbish they ate, it was a miracle they were able to keep body and soul together. Snails, for God's sake. Horsemeat. He shuddered.

"So when do you reckon we should do it?"

Dave had another swig of beer and wiped his mouth with the back of his hand. "Best would be after work, when he goes out for his dinner. When it's dark."

They left the pub and walked back to the van, pausing from time to time to consider the range of bikes on display. It was as

Dave had said. Bikes were everywhere—BMWs, Kawasakis, Hondas, Ducatis, even a highly polished Harley—and they had been left in places consistent with the cavalier French habit of parking wherever you please, regardless of regulations.

"We don't want anything too flash," said Dave. "Nothing that anyone would remember. And we'll have to muddy up the number plates." He ran his hand over a nearby Yamaha and patted the saddle. "Right. Here's what we'll do. Tonight, around two o'clock when it's nice and quiet, we'll nick the bikes and load 'em in the van. Tomorrow night we'll do the job and dump the bikes. Piece of cake."

Brian nodded. "Piece of cake, Dave."


Philippe was working late, putting the final touches to the article he had spent the afternoon writing. His brush with Ray Prendergast still rankled, and this had caused him to be more than normally enthusiastic about Sam's idea of putting a tent on the beach. It was, so he wrote, a breath of fresh air blowing into the murky, secretive, and often corrupt world of urban development. He went on to add to the complimentary remarks he'd already made about Sam's project in a previous article, and finished off with a question: Would the other two projects show similar imagination, or was it going to be business as usual behind closed doors?

He leaned back in his chair, rubbed his eyes, and looked at his watch. An evening of duty lay ahead—the monthly dinner with Elodie and Raoul, Mimi's parents. If this followed its normal course, there would be discreet questions about his career prospects and a gentle hint or two about getting rid of his scooter, buying a car, and, as Elodie always put it, "settling down." It was a source of constant surprise to Philippe that this implacably bourgeois couple could ever have produced an unconventional daughter like Mimi. He remembered when she had dyed her hair that wonderful deep red. The parental shock—and barely concealed disapproval—had lasted for weeks. Ah, well. They were basically good, kind people, and Elodie was a magnificent cook. Philippe decided to have a shave in her honor and take her a bunch of roses.

Elena was packing. Sam had learned over the years and on many occasions that this was a sensitive ritual, never to be disturbed. Elena didn't like to be watched when she was packing. She didn't like to be helped. Most of all, she didn't like to be talked to. Her relationship with her suitcase and its contents was one of mystical communion, and woe betide anyone who broke the spell. So Sam had decided to make himself scarce with a book in the living room.

Elena was off to Paris for two or three days, the result of a long and deeply apologetic phone call from her boss, Frank Knox. The Paris office was having a problem with its most important client, the CEO of a group of luxury hotels. He felt neglected, above all by the Knox head office. He felt he needed reassurance about the quality of service he was getting. He felt, in a word, unloved. Would it be possible, Frank had asked, for Elena to go up to Paris and smooth his ruffled feathers? If it seemed as though she had come all the way from Los Angeles just to have a chat with him over dinner, so much the better. In return, Frank had said, he would insist on Elena extending her vacation by an extra week. On hearing the news, Sam had been very understanding. He was going to be busy over the next few days anyway, and her return would be a good excuse to celebrate.

He got up and went over to put his ear against the bedroom door. He was just able to make out the sound of the shower coming from Elena's bathroom, always a sure sign that the challenges of packing had been successfully overcome. He went through to the kitchen and opened a bottle of the Domaine Ott *rosé* that Reboul had left for them. Carrying two glasses, he arrived back in the living room just as Elena, wet-haired and wrapped in a towel, came through the opposite door.

"All done?" Sam asked.

"All done." Elena took a sip of her wine and put down her glass. "You know you said we could celebrate when I got back? Well . . ." She unwrapped the towel and let it drop to the floor. "How about a rehearsal?"

# *Eleven*

"Will you miss me?"

Elena, dressed for the city in business black, was waiting for the early-evening flight to Paris to be called, and she and Sam were having a cup of coffee at the airport bar.

"How am I going to survive?" Sam's hand, under the table, stroked her silken knee. "Seriously, I'd love to be coming with you, but there's all kinds of stuff to get ready before the presentation. You know me—a slave to my work. I can't resist a cozy evening with my laptop."

Elena smiled. "Mimi taught me this great word the other day. *Blagueur.* Describes you perfectly."

"It doesn't sound good. What does it mean?"

"Joker. Kidder. Someone who's full of it."

"I'll take that as a compliment." Sam looked up at the departures board. "You'd better get going. Give my love to Paris."

A kiss, a wave, and she was gone.

• • •

Philippe took a final look at the piece he'd just finished, pressed the key that would send it through to the copy desk, and leaned back in his chair. This, for him, was one of the most satisfying moments of his job. Tomorrow, the words he had written would be history, but tonight, they still looked fresh—clear, incisive, well argued, with one or two touches of humor. He allowed himself a mental pat on the back. He had a couple of calls to make, and then he would be done for the day.

It was late, almost nine o'clock, by the time he went downstairs to pick up his scooter from the parking garage.

Reboul answered his phone on the third ring.

"Francis? Sam—I hope I'm not calling at a bad time?"

"Not at all, Sam, not at all. I'm all alone with a pile of papers from my accountant." A gusty sigh came down the phone. "Business! One of these days I'm going to give it up, move to one of those shacks on the beach, find a brown-skinned girl, and become a fisherman."

"Sure you will. And I'm going to enter a monastery. Meanwhile, I have a bit of good news: Philippe just called. He's done what sounds like a useful piece about our presentation: 'A Tent on the Anse des Pêcheurs' is the headline. It's going to be in the paper later this week."

"Good. That should make Patrimonio's day. Has he fixed the date for the presentation yet?"

"End of next week, so Gaston has plenty of time to set everything up."

"What did you think of him?"

"Gaston? A total rogue."

Reboul chuckled. "You're right. But don't forget, my dear Sam, he's *our* rogue. Let me know if you have any problems, *d'accord?* Oh, and Sam? I thought it would be amusing to celebrate the presentation with a little dinner—very quiet, just the four of us. I'd like you to meet my new friend."

Let's hope we have something to celebrate, Sam thought as he put the phone down. Both Reboul and Philippe seemed to think the result was a foregone conclusion, but Sam wasn't so sure. Wapping was a tough opponent, and Patrimonio was no fool. They weren't about to give up quickly.

Restless and already missing Elena, Sam tried her number. Her phone was switched off. By now, she was probably sitting in some pompous restaurant with her client, doing her best to appear fascinated by his description of the problems of running a chain of hotels. Not for the first time, Sam thought how lucky he was to have a life that offered so much variety and so little routine. Consoled by this, he poured himself a glass of wine and went back to his presentation.

The atmosphere in the master's cabin of *The Floating Pound* was not as convivial as usual. Lord Wapping was somewhat on edge. His spies had been picking up altogether too many favorable comments made by the committee about Sam's proposal. And so Patrimonio had been summoned for a council of war.

"I don't like what I'm hearing, Jérôme. All this rubbish about a breath of fresh air, something for the people of Marseille—well, you've heard it all, I'm sure. It's got to stop. Can't you tell those blokes on the committee to put a cork in it?"

Wapping's vocabulary often puzzled Patrimonio, but this time the sense was clear. His Lordship wanted his hand held. Patrimonio shot his cuffs, smoothed back his hair, and put on his most reassuring smile. "Oh, I don't think we need to worry. I know these men, and they know I'll take care of them. Let them have their say. In the end they will come to their senses. In any case, it's votes that count, not a few remarks made for the benefit of the public. And votes, we must remember, are cast in secret."

Wapping was sufficiently encouraged to pour two glasses of Krug from the bottle that stood in a crystal bucket at his elbow. Patrimonio took a first sip, raised his eyebrows in approval, and leaned forward, a frown on his face. It was his turn to be reassured. "There is a small concern." He shrugged, as if to show how small it was. "That little *salaud* of a journalist. I hope we can be sure he won't be writing any more of his nonsense, and I remember you said he would be taken care of."

Wapping looked at him in silence for a moment. "As I said to you the other day, I don't think you want to hear any details."

Patrimonio sat back in his chair and fluttered a manicured

hand. "No, no. It's just . . ." His voice tailed off, and he dived back into his champagne.

"Good." Wapping raised his glass. "Well then. Here's to a well-deserved success."

Five minutes later, Patrimonio was in a boat taxi heading back to Marseille.

Ray Prendergast, although not a gourmet by nature, had recently begun to look forward to his meals with increased interest. France was all very well for some people, he thought, but not for him. Quite apart from the irritating babble of the language, he had a problem with French food. It was always mucked about with—all those sauces and bits and pieces, a man didn't know what he was eating. And then, a few days ago, someone had told him about Geoffrey's of Antibes. It had come as a truly life-changing revelation.

Geoffrey's was an emporium—no other word could do it justice—dedicated to the particular taste buds of hungry expatriates homesick for British grub. All the traditional favorites of British cuisine were there: bacon, proper sausages, baked beans, pork pies, beef curry. There was blue Stilton, there was Old Speckled Hen beer. There was even porridge, and McVitie's Chocolate Digestive biscuits. And when he learned that the maritime division of Geoffrey's provided a boat delivery service, Ray Prendergast thought that fate had indeed smiled upon him.

He was just settling down with a bacon sandwich and a pornographic DVD that had been lent to him by Tiny de Salis when his phone rang. Lord Wapping had a couple of questions.

"You've been missing a lot of meals lately, Ray. Chef's worried about you. You all right?"

"Better than ever, Billy." He was halfway through an enthusiastic account of his new gastronomic discovery when Wapping cut him short.

"Some other time, Ray. What I need to know now is where we stand with that little tosser of a journalist. What's happening?"

"Well, the lads have done their homework, they're tooled up, and they're waiting for the right moment. Timing is everything, know what I mean? But Dave did say that tonight could be the night. He's going to call me when it's done. I'll let you know as soon as I hear."

Wapping nodded. "You do that, Ray. Oh, this bloke Geoffrey that you're so keen on. Does he do kippers?"

"There he is." Moving as one, Brian and Dave pulled down the visors of their crash helmets and kicked their bikes into life. They had spent the evening waiting for Philippe to leave the office. Tonight he was later than usual, which Brian and Dave thought was a good omen. The Frogs would all be at the trough having dinner, there would be less traffic on the roads, and so it would be easier to keep an eye on their victim from a distance.

Staying about a hundred yards behind him, they followed Philippe as he cut through a tangle of back streets and alleys that eventually led to the Vieux Port. This was the crucial moment. Was he going out to dinner somewhere in the crowded center of the city, or was he going home along the less busy Corniche?

He headed south along the side of the Vieux Port, then kept going straight. Brian and Dave exchanged a thumbs-up; he was heading home.

The air was still quite warm, and the breeze coming in from the sea had a pleasantly salty smell. The Corniche was hardly deserted—it never was—but traffic was light, and Philippe relaxed in his saddle, pleased that for once he didn't have to dodge too many lunatic, scooter-hating motorists.

He heard the sound of an engine behind him, and glanced across at the big Kawasaki as it passed. It moved over until it was directly in front of him, and slowed down. Then he heard another engine closing in, and saw a second bike in his rearview mirror. And that's when he knew he was in trouble. He was now the filling in the sandwich. It was the classic hijacker's setup. His underpowered scooter had no chance of getting away.

The next few moments passed in a blur. The bike behind him drew level with him and closed in until it was almost touching the scooter. Brian's size-twelve boot thumped into Philippe's knee, throwing the scooter off balance, unseating Philippe, and sending him skidding across the Corniche. His last conscious thought was that he should have worn his crash helmet. After that, darkness.

• • •

"Nice one," said Dave. "I thought that went off very well." They were back in their rented van after leaving the bikes neatly parked behind the Gare Marseille Saint-Charles, Marseille's principal railroad station. "I'd better call Ray and put him out of his misery."

"It's all done and dusted, Raymond. A good, neat job. No witnesses."

"What was the damage?"

Dave rolled his eyes. "I didn't stop to ask him, did I? But he's not going to be playing football for a few weeks, that's for sure."

Lord Wapping received the news with satisfaction, tinged with relief. He needed something to cheer him up after a day when the banks had been peppering him with e-mails. They had become more and more insistent, and all with the same depressing message: Where's our money? We need our money. Wapping would have loved to tell them to shove it, but he had nowhere to go. It was too late to raise that kind of money anywhere else. He sat there brooding over his champagne. He had started off as the favorite, and he and Patrimonio had done all they could to sweeten the committee's pie. Even so, he had the nagging feeling that this particular race was in danger of going to the outsider, the American and his bloody beach huts.

Back in his old bookmaking days, there had usually been

a chance to fix the result of a race. Jockeys—some of them, at least—had been known to accept a discreet bribe. Horses, delicate creatures that they were, could be made to feel out of sorts on race day, with the cooperation of a helpful stable lad. One way or another, the performance of a promising outsider could sometimes be adjusted to meet the needs of business. It was called *nobbling*.

Wapping stared out at the blackness of the Mediterranean, turning this over in his mind.

By the time Sam closed his laptop it was almost midnight. Too late, he decided, to call Elena. And so her call came as a pleasant surprise.

"Sam, I hope I didn't wake you, but after this evening I need some light relief."

"That bad, was it?"

"Worse. Dinner was just one long monologue. Then he wanted to go dancing at Castel. Sam, what is it with short men?"

"What do you mean?"

"I've noticed it before. They're like climbing plants. Hands everywhere."

It reminded Sam of the old story about Mickey Rooney, who was famously short and famously attracted to very tall women. He shared the story with Elena. Many years ago, in Paris, Rooney was introduced to one of the Bluebell Girls, the troupe of dancers noted for their beauty and their statuesque proportions. Mickey was instantly smitten.

"You're sensational," he said to the girl. "Oh God, how I'd like to make love to you."

The Bluebell Girl looked down on him from her considerable height (she was six foot four in heels). "Well, if you do," she said, "and I ever find out about it, you'll be in serious trouble."

Elena laughed. "Thanks, Sam. I needed that. Luckily, he has to be in Berlin tomorrow afternoon. We have a morning meeting, and then I'm out of here. Can't wait."

# Twelve

Philippe opened one bleary eye, and flinched. Everything was bright and white, including the nurse who was bending over him.

"How do we feel?" Her voice had that optimistic perkiness nurses adopt when they're sure that the patient won't die on their shift.

Philippe considered the question. He was warm, comfortable, relaxed, free of pain, almost floating. He grinned at the nurse. "We feel terrific."

"That's the morphine. You've had a bad accident, but you've been very lucky. You hit a lamppost, and that stopped you going over the edge of the Corniche. You've broken a couple of ribs, and you have multiple lacerations and a black eye, but that's all."

"That's all?"

"It could have been much worse. Now then. Drink this. Dr. Joel will be coming to see you in a few minutes. There's a phone on your bedside table if you want to call anyone."

Philippe called Mimi, Mimi called Elena, and by the time Dr. Joel had come and gone, the two of them, plus Sam, were gathered around his bed.

"*Mon pauvre garçon,*" said Mimi, kissing the tip of Philippe's nose. "Whatever happened? Were you . . . ?" She brought her fist up to her mouth, thumb extended, the classic gesture that is shorthand for too much to drink.

Philippe shook his head gingerly. "I hadn't touched a drop, honestly—not even a glass of *rosé*. Two bikes boxed me in, one in front, one behind. And then, *paf!*, a kick in the knee knocked me off the scooter. I'm sure it was a professional job, but God knows why they did it. I don't think they stole anything—there was nothing to steal—so perhaps it was just for a bit of fun."

"Would you recognize them if you saw them again?"

Another tentative shake of the head. "Not a chance. They had the visors on their helmets pulled down."

Sam was frowning. In his experience, professionals didn't do anything for fun. These two had meant to teach Philippe a lesson, perhaps even kill him. But why? Who would gain if he were out of action? It didn't take long to come to the obvious conclusion. "When is that piece on the tent coming out?"

"Tomorrow," said Mimi. "The editor loved it."

"So it couldn't have been that. But your first article didn't go down too well with some people—Patrimonio, for one. And you had that row with him at the cocktail party. Even so, that's not reason enough to take someone out. No, it wouldn't be Patrimonio; it has to be Wapping. He's in bed with Patrimonio, and he tried to bribe you to shut you up. It has to be him."

Philippe fixed Sam with his one good eye. "OK. That makes sense. And I'll tell you something: If the first piece made him furious, tomorrow's piece will give him a heart attack." He turned to Mimi, and grinned. "Do you think the paper will spring for a bodyguard?"

"I have a better idea," said Sam. "I think you should disappear."

"Sam, you've been reading too many thrillers. Besides, I'm not going to stop working just because of that *connard*."

"You won't have to stop working. You just won't be working in your office, in your apartment, or anywhere else you normally go, because then you'd be a sitting duck for Wapping's goons. You're going to vanish from all your old haunts. You're going to come and live with us."

Sam held up his hand before Philippe could interrupt. "It's perfect. There's plenty of room. The house is secluded and protected; it couldn't be safer. There's a car and driver whenever you need them, there's a housekeeper, a maid, and us to look after you. As I said, it's perfect. I don't want an argument. How soon can we get you out of here?"

Dr. Joel was consulted and he eventually agreed, on the condition that a nurse come in every day to check on Philippe and change his dressings. Olivier the driver met them at the hospital entrance, while Mimi went off to collect a few clothes from Philippe's apartment. By the time the good people of Marseille were sitting down to lunch, Olivier and his passengers were making their way through the double gates leading to the house.

"This is bizarre," said Philippe. "I think I know this place." He nodded once or twice as he looked around. "In fact, I'm sure I know it. A few years ago—it must have been a flat time for news—the paper did a big feature on the homes of Marseille's rich and famous. This was one of them. It used to belong to Reboul before he bought Le Pharo. Maybe it still does." He looked at Sam, his face made slightly sinister by his black eye. "So how did you find it?"

For a few days now, Sam had been feeling increasingly uncomfortable that he had hidden his connection with Reboul from Philippe. He decided it was time to come clean. "We need to have a chat," he said, "but not on an empty stomach. It's a long story. Let's leave it until after lunch."

Alas, that proved to be too much of a wait for Philippe. A man desperate for a nap, he only just missed falling asleep in his dessert. It wasn't until the early evening, *l'heure du pastis,* that they settled down on the terrace. Sam collected his thoughts and started at the beginning.

Philippe was fascinated. It was a story within a story, and it was only with the greatest reluctance that he agreed to keep Reboul's name out of the articles he was planning to write.

For the time being, anyway. "Once this is over," said Sam,

"I can guarantee you an interview with Reboul. Exclusive. Do we have a deal?"

Philippe reached over to shake hands. "We have a deal."

"Actually, I'm sure you'll like him."

Philippe shook his head and grinned. "I never met an exclusive I didn't like."

The following morning, reactions to Philippe's article were predictably mixed.

Philippe himself enjoyed a few moments of modest satisfaction. For once, he didn't want to rewrite the piece as soon as he saw it in type. It was flagged on the front page, and took up most of page three. The tone was informative and concise, with the occasional graceful turn of phrase, and the artist's impression of the tent on the beach needed only a few topless sunbathers to look just like Saint-Tropez. Not bad. Not bad at all.

Sam was looking over Philippe's shoulder as he read. "Nobody's going to miss that," he said. "But I don't think Patrimonio will be sending you a Christmas card this year."

The piece had already ruined Patrimonio's breakfast, and was doing the same to his entire morning. Members of the committee had been calling to express their opinions, and they were almost all favorable. "Good to see a little imagination" was mentioned more than once, as was that old standby, "a breath of fresh air." The only minor criticism came from the committee's oldest member, a veteran in his eighties, who complained that there was no mention of toilet facilities, a subject of particular interest to him. But on the whole, it was seen as an enthusiastic endorsement of Sam's idea.

Patrimonio's call to Wapping was short, loud, and hostile.

"I thought you said you were taking care of that *salaud* of a journalist?"

Wapping bristled. He wasn't used to being shouted at. "What are you talking about? The boys sorted him out the night before last."

"Have you seen this morning's paper?"

"Why? What about it?"

"*C'est une catastrophe.* Call me when you've read it."

Elena swept out of the bedroom and performed a twirl so that Sam could appreciate her dress—summery, flimsy, almost diaphanous. "Worth the wait," he said. "Well worth the wait. Are you ready?"

Sam had promised to celebrate Elena's return from Paris with lunch overlooking the sea. But first, there was a little business: a rendezvous with Gaston on the beach, where the tent was being put up in preparation for the presentation.

Gaston saw them as they arrived and waddled across the beach to greet them. By now, Sam was used to the effusions of gallantry that Elena inspired in French men, and Gaston was no exception. Cradling Elena's hand in both of his, he raised it to his lips like a thirsty man reaching out for water. While one hand continued to hold hers, the other began a slow, smooth movement up her arm, which would doubtless have continued if Elena hadn't giggled.

"What a delightful surprise," said Gaston. "I was expecting only Sam." And then, with a wink directed at Elena, "Come with me to my tent."

As they walked inside, Sam was struck by the warm, golden glow made by the sun filtering through white canvas. If the presentation was held as planned in the early evening there would be no need for artificial light. "Once the floor's down, this is going to look great," he said. "But suppose people start dropping in off the street and having a party?"

"*Pas de soucis.* I've arranged security—two big boys, Jules and Jim, and two Rottweilers. They'll be here every night." Gaston led them over to the far side of the tent. "Here is where I think the bar should be. You see? If you turn around and look through the entrance over there, you'll be able to watch the sun set as you drink your champagne. What could be more agreeable?"

As Gaston's guided tour continued, Sam relaxed. The details had been taken care of. Everything from the size and positioning of the bar to the provision for electricity if needed, from the conference table and chairs to notepads and pencils—it had all been thought through and dealt with. There was even a small but elegant *cabinet de toilette* tucked away behind the tent.

Gaston waved aside Sam's congratulations. "*C'est normal,* my friend. And now, although it breaks my heart to say *au revoir* to mademoiselle, I must leave you. I have a lunch appointment with my friend the mayor."

Back on the Corniche, they stopped so that Elena could slip off her shoes and shake out the sand. "What did you think of our new partner in crime?" asked Sam.

"Gaston? He's cute," she said. "And I'm starving. How far is lunch?"

"Just up the road."

Peron is one of those restaurants you dream about in the depths of a cold, dark winter. It is suspended high above the Mediterranean, facing south, and so the urban clutter of cranes, buildings, and power lines is nowhere to be seen. The view is pure, shining sea, its surface ruffled from time to time by the wake of the occasional small boat. In the distance is the miniature archipelago of the Frioul islands, gray-green at midday, turning purple at sunset. And when you tear yourself away from the view, there is the food—fish of every local variety caught that morning and cooked by one of the best chefs on the coast.

Feeling as though they had left dry land and stepped onto the deck of a spacious, immobile boat, Elena and Sam followed the hostess as she led them toward the corner of the terrace. A bellow of English coming from a large group nearby announced the presence of Lord Wapping, seated at his regular table, surrounded by his regular entourage of hangers-on. The group fell silent as Elena and Sam passed. Sam exchanged nods with Wapping, who turned to watch them as they reached their table, his expression malevolent.

"What a pretty girl, sweetie, don't you think?" said Annabel. "Although perhaps not—she's a little ethnic for you, with that rather suspect dark skin and all that black hair. You prefer us English roses, don't you." There was a grunt from Wapping, the sound of a laugh from the end of the table, and conversation resumed.

After their first chilled sip of Cassis, Elena and Sam turned their attention to the menu, which Elena discovered was filled with exotic names that she had never seen in Los Angeles: *pagre* and *rascasse*, *rouget* and *daurade*. And then her eye was caught by the *véritable bouillabaisse de Marseille*, the legendary "golden soup."

"Have you ever had that, Sam?"

"Last time I was in Marseille, with Philippe. He's a *bouillabaisse* addict—he spent the entire dinner telling me about it. It's good. Kind of messy, but good."

"What's in it, exactly?"

"Pretty much anything that swims in the Mediterranean: John Dory, conger eel, scorpion fish, sea hen, lots more. Then you have tomatoes, potatoes, onions, garlic, saffron, olive oil, parsley. And then there's the *rouille*—that's a kind of thick, spicy mayonnaise, with more garlic, more saffron, more olive oil, and hot peppers. And last, you need thin slices of toasted *baguette*. Oh, and an oversized napkin to cover you from the neck down. Try it. You'll like it."

Elena was not too sure. "Well . . ."

"There's a bonus. As this is the first time you've had it, you're entitled to a wish."

"Will you still find me irresistible when I reek of garlic?"

"I'm having it too. We'll reek together."

Helped by their waiter, Elena adjusted her napkin until she felt she was safe from attacks by flying *rouille*, and watched as the ingredients were laid out in front of her.

"Allow me," said Sam. He took a small slice of *baguette*, spread it with thick, dark-red *rouille*, and soaked it in the soup until the bread was soft and thoroughly moist. "You ready?"

Elena leaned forward, opened her mouth, and closed her eyes.

She chewed, she swallowed, her eyes opened wide. "Mmm," she said. "More."

One minor drawback of *bouillabaisse* is that it takes up so much of the eaters' concentrated attention that simple speech is often difficult, let alone the cut and thrust of spirited conversation. And so this first part of their meal passed with little more than small sounds of pleasure. It wasn't until the debris had been cleared away and fresh napkins provided that they could lean back and talk to one another again.

Sam was the first to break the contented silence. "Have you made that wish?"

"Right now? I think my wish would be to stay like this, a long way away from the insurance business, crooked clients, pompous executives, endless meetings, L.A. smog, desk lunches—in other words, away from real life." She put down the menu she'd been studying, and grinned. "But for the time being, I'll settle for the black-and-white ice cream."

They lingered over their coffee, watching the seagulls swooping low over the terrace in search of scraps. A long, sunny afternoon lay ahead, and they were comparing the merits of a boat trip to the *calanques* with the lure of the pool when Sam's phone rang.

Real life was on the line, in the form of Jérôme Patrimonio's secretary. It was necessary, so she said, for Sam to come *at once* to the office for an urgent and important meeting with Monsieur Patrimonio. Sam sighed and shook his head as he put down the phone. He had probably forgotten to dot an *i* or cross a *t* on one of the seemingly endless documents that had to be presented with the bid.

But when he arrived at Patrimonio's office, the great man clearly had more pressing matters on his mind, and Sam had barely taken his seat before Patrimonio shot his cuffs and got down to business.

"This affair of the tent," he said. "It is, I'm afraid, unacceptable. Completely unacceptable. We cannot have Marseille's public spaces used to promote commercial interests."

"Why not?" said Sam. "This is a development that will benefit the city and the people who live here."

"That may be so. But you must agree that you are trying to create an unfair advantage for yourself over the other two bidders."

"I thought that's what business was all about. In any case, there is nothing to stop them using other public spaces for their presentations—the O.M. stadium, for instance. Or La Vieille Charité, which I seem to remember you yourself used."

Patrimonio shot his cuffs with a violence that threatened to rip his shirtsleeves off. "Altogether different," he said. "And you have chosen to ignore the crucial matter of permissions."

He sat back in his chair and nodded with considerable emphasis, as though he had just scored a definitive victory. "Without my permission, this scheme of yours cannot go ahead. *Point final*. And now, if you'll excuse me, I have another meeting."

Sam resisted the impulse to shoot his own cuffs in reply. "You didn't give me the chance to tell you," he said. "But I do have permission. From the mayor. Your boss."

# Thirteen

"I don't believe this. He's got permission from the mayor? Have you checked?" Lord Wapping took his half-smoked cigar—a Cohiba, he liked to tell people, fifteen quid apiece—and crushed it to death in the ashtray.

"It's true," said Patrimonio. "I regret infinitely, but there's nothing I can do about it."

"As per bloody usual. And I thought you had the whole thing sewn up. But no. First the journalist and now this. What about the mayor? Is he for sale?"

Patrimonio thought about the mayor's irreproachable record, his constant efforts to reduce crime, his loathing of corruption. "I think it would be most unwise to try anything with the mayor. That would immediately destroy our chances."

"What about that other place? Have you got that sorted out?"

"Of course. No problem."

"That makes a change." Wapping put down the phone and tried to relight the remains of his cigar. As soon as he had heard about the tent on the beach, he had told Patrimonio to find an equally unusual setting for his presentation, and a renovated grain silo down near the port had been suggested. It wouldn't attract the publicity of the tent, but it was certainly better than the Parisian team's choice of the conference room in a Marseille hotel, where their presentation was being held that afternoon.

His Lordship brooded. He was running out of time, and he was running out of excuses to fend off the banks. Desperate measures were called for. He summoned Ray Prendergast, and went over the situation with him.

Prendergast listened and nodded, looking more than ever like an attentive gnome. "What we have here, Billy," he said as Wapping finished his tale of woe, "is an opportunity to think outside the box. Now then, when is Levitt's presentation? Day after tomorrow, right? So there's not time to start all over again if an accident should happen."

"Who to?"

"Not who to, Billy. Not this time. I was thinking of something more along the lines of a natural catastrophe—Brian and Dave and a box of matches. Very careless with the matches, our Dave. And what happens? Guy Fawkes's night with all the fireworks, that's what. Whoops, the tent goes up in flames, and so does the presentation."

The idea appealed to Wapping instantly. It was crude, simple, and menacing, like some of the stunts he'd pulled in the old days. Besides, time was short and there weren't many options. He nodded. "All right, Ray. We'll give it a go. Wait until the last minute—tomorrow night. Don't let them have a chance to find another tent."

In addition to all his other responsibilities, Gaston had been given the task of finding an interpreter to help with Sam's presentation. Most of the project committee spoke some English, but Sam was anxious that nobody should miss any important details.

Two candidates had survived Gaston's selection process, and Sam had arranged to interview them at the house. Elena was standing by, more out of curiosity than a sense of duty, to welcome the two hopefuls. The first was a young Frenchwoman in her twenties, Mademoiselle Silvestre, and it was instantly clear why Gaston had picked her. Despite the black dress and the attaché case, there was more than a hint of the bedroom about her, accentuated by her perfume, the height of her heels, and the elaborate way in which she adjusted her skirt and crossed her legs after she'd sat down.

Sam swallowed hard and started to go through his list of questions. Yes, she was bilingual, and yes, she was available for the evening of the presentation. When he asked her how she had learned to speak such good English, she smiled.

"Perhaps you'd like to see my curriculum vitae," she said, making it sound more like an invitation to a romp than a question. She took the papers from her attaché case and leaned over to pass them to Sam, treating him to a heady whiff of perfume and a most unbusinesslike panorama of bosom.

"Looks good," he said. "I'll read this and get back to you."

Elena came back after showing her out. "That's the kind of girl who would sit on your lap to take dictation."

"How can you tell?"

Elena sniffed. "Women know these things. The other one's just arrived. *Much* more suitable."

Miss Perkins, a regal woman of a certain age, had worked in the liaison department of the British Consulate in Marseille for twenty years before it was shut down. She wore a starched white blouse fastened at the neck with a cameo brooch, and what she would describe as a sensible skirt and shoes. She immediately took charge of the interview.

"Would you prefer that we talked in English or in French? I imagine you're more comfortable if we use English."

"You're right. Let's do that. I guess Gaston will have told you what we need? The project committee is not all that fluent in English, and I'd like our presentation to be as clear and professional as possible. That will obviously impact their decision."

A pained expression appeared on Miss Perkins's pink face. "If you will forgive my saying so, 'impact' is a noun. In correct English, it is never used as a verb. Rather like the persistent misuse of 'hopefully,' I'm afraid it is one of the many infelicities committed by our American friends." A sweet smile took the sting out of her words. "Now then, dear. I shall need to have the text of your presentation so that I can make a written translation we can leave with the members of the committee. I hope that will be possible?"

"Of course, Miss Perkins."

She held up a plump hand. "Please, dear. Call me Daphne. After all, we are going to be working together."

Sam joined Elena outside the house to see Miss Perkins safely into her tiny car, a classic 2CV, and watched it clatter out through the gates.

"You were right," said Sam. "Much more suitable. In fact, I didn't have a chance. She just took over, which is fine with me. You know how I adore strong women."

Elena rolled her eyes, but said nothing.

They went back into the house, to find Philippe clutching his ribs and pacing up and down as he finished talking on his cell phone. As he turned toward them, they could see that his eye, once black, was turning a mottled, jaundiced yellow. "That was Étienne," he said, "my contact at police headquarters. He did me a favor and went through the log for the past few days. Two bikes were reported stolen the night I got hit—which is exactly what professionals would have done. They never use their own wheels. Here," he said, opening his laptop, "take a look at this." He read it out to them in English.

The headline on the screen got the piece off to a dramatic start: "MY BRUSH WITH DEATH ON THE CORNICHE," and the text began by describing the attack in clinical detail, concluding that it had been a skilled, professional job. Philippe then went on to speculate. He had been careful to avoid mentioning names, restricting himself to questions: Why had this happened at this particular time? Who was behind it? What was their motive? And in the end, a few stirring words about an attack on a journalist being an attack on the freedom of the press.

"Well? What do you think?" Philippe closed the laptop and patted it. "Could you take a mug shot to go with the piece before the eye clears up?"

Elena was shaking her head. "I don't know, Philippe. Are you sure about this? These guys aren't playing games."

"I think Philippe's right," said Sam. "They shouldn't be allowed to get away with something like this. If Wapping's behind it, and we're pretty sure he is, he'll be gone and back in England within a few days. As long as Philippe stays here, he'll be safe. And who knows? Perhaps this kind of publicity will make Wapping behave himself. It might even help the police."

Elena fetched her camera and photographed Philippe posing in front of a plain white wall, doing his best to look grim and disfigured. Sam looked at the image on the camera's tiny screen, then showed it to Philippe. "Terrific. You look like a corpse. Tell the guys at the paper not to retouch a thing."

Reboul was back in Marseille after a few days of business in London. Sam's call was answered by a long-drawn-out grunt that could have been either pain or pleasure before Reboul's voice took over. "Sorry about that, Sam. I'm having a massage, and she has thumbs of steel, this masseuse."

"How was your trip?"

"A little strange. There were times when I thought I was still in France. You know, there are between three and four hundred thousand French living in London now. There's a sort of expensive ghetto in South Kensington they call La Vallée des Grenouilles—Frog Valley—and parts of London are just like Paris with bad weather. How the world has changed. Now tell me—what's been happening?"

Reboul listened quietly to an account of the events of the past few days, taking particular pleasure from Sam's interview with Patrimonio. There was just the occasional murmured *"très bien"* by way of interruption until Sam came to the subject of Philippe.

"You mean you told him everything? This journalist? Is he discreet? Most of them aren't."

"He guaranteed to keep your name out of it until the moment when you step in with rescue financing. I know him well. He's on our side, I promise you. Trust me."

"The two most dangerous words in the language. But"— Sam could almost hear the shrug at the other end of the line— "what's done is done. You trust him and I trust you."

Sam put down the phone with a silent prayer that Philippe would be as good as his word. It would be difficult, he knew, for him to keep quiet, to suppress the journalist's visceral urge to be first with the news, but Sam was sure that Philippe was that rarity, an honorable man.

One more call, this time to Miss Perkins. Did she have everything she needed for the presentation? He needn't have worried.

"I've nearly finished translating your speech, dear. Very nice, in spite of one or two rather curious words and phrases— 'lifestyle' and so forth. But then, you're American. In any case, everything will be ready to be printed and bound tomorrow morning. This is all quite exciting, isn't it? Do you think it might be helpful if I came to the presentation, just in case there are complications with the French?"

"Daphne, I wouldn't dream of trying to do it without you."

"Very well, dear. Tomorrow it is. I'll be with you about midday with the presentation documents. Now be sure to get a good night's rest."

It was three in the morning, and Brian and Dave had no trouble finding a spot to park their rented car just above the beach. Without leaving their seats, they could see the tent fifty yards away, and the faint glow of light coming from one end.

"You reckon there's someone in there?"

"Bound to be. Some old geezer, probably."

"Suppose he's having a kip?"

"Well, this will wake him up, won't it? We'll start at the dark end. That'll give him time to hop it. Right. Off we go."

They got out of the car and looked up and down the deserted stretch of the Corniche before opening the trunk and taking out two twenty-liter jerricans of kerosene and two gas firelighters. Down the steps and onto the beach, their feet made no sound in the sand. They were just about to fan out on either side of the tent when Brian stopped. He turned to Dave, close enough to whisper.

"What's that noise?"

They stood in the darkness, listening intently. They could hear a low, continuous rumble coming from inside the tent.

"They must have a generator in there."

The rumbling became louder as the tent flap was pushed open, and two dark shapes came out onto the beach.

"Bloody hell." Dave had forgotten to whisper. The Rottweilers heard the sound and started in their direction, wary and now silent. Without thinking, Dave and Brian dropped the jerricans and made for the steps that would take them off the beach, only to find that the dogs had circled around to block their escape. The two men retreated. The Rottweilers followed them down toward the sea, as intent and disciplined as sheepdogs patrolling their flock.

"Do you know about dogs, Dave? Can they swim?"

The dogs quickened their pace, and as they came closer there was an impressive show of teeth glinting in the moonlight. Brian and Dave waited no longer. They turned and hurled themselves into the water, where they spent a cold and nervous half hour putting as much distance as possible between themselves and the dogs.

Jules, whose turn it was to spend the night on guard duty, whistled the dogs back and gave them each a biscuit. Walking around the tent, he found the jerricans. Perhaps there would be fingerprints on them. But to hell with it. They'd still be there tomorrow. He stretched and yawned. He'd call the police in the morning.

The day had started early and badly for Lord Wapping, with the sodden and shamefaced Brian and Dave having to confess complete failure, and it wasn't long before there was another dose of unpleasant news. Ray Prendergast had received an e-mail from Hoffman and Myers, the private bank that was Wapping's biggest creditor, and it made uncomfortable reading.

"They're well pissed off, Billy. Not only that. They're sending two of their heavies over to Marseille to sort things out, 'following your unsatisfactory response to our previous communications.' That's what they said."

"Bastards. How's a man expected to make an honest living with all this interference? Did they say when they were coming?"

"That's a bit of a problem, Billy. They're going to be here tomorrow unless we can put them off."

Wapping got up from his desk and paced over to the nearest porthole. His presentation was scheduled for three days' time, and his only chance was to keep the bankers at bay until that was over. He looked out to sea, which was as flat as a board. The sun was up, there was no wind: a perfect cruising day.

He turned back to Prendergast. "Right," he said. "Send them an e-mail. Tell them I'm at sea for a few days, and can't be reached. Regrets, best wishes, all that crap. And tell Tiny to get the boat ready to go as quickly as possible, OK?"

"Where are we off to, sweetie?" asked Annabel, who could never resist an open door and the chance to eavesdrop. She had appeared in the doorway draped in a towel, her hair still wet from the pool. "Can I put in a tiny request for Saint-Tropez? Sir Frank is there for the summer, and so are the Escobars from Argentina. *Such* fun."

• • •

Miss Perkins had arrived as promised with the presentation documents, and had agreed to stay for lunch. Philippe, looking less jaundiced by the day, had been joined by Mimi. Sam was bringing the barbecue to a healthy glow, Elena was tossing the salad, the *rosé* was chilling nicely, and the mood around the big table under the parasol pines was good-humored and optimistic.

There is something about eating outside on a fine warm day that brings out the *raconteur* in people. They sit back. They relax. They feel expansive. It soon became apparent that Miss Perkins had plenty of stories to tell, from her schooldays at Roedean, which she described as "a temple of learning for wayward middle-class girls," to some highly indiscreet revelations about life in the British Consulate. Time passed quickly, and on glancing at his watch Sam was surprised to see that it was already two-thirty. They needed to go. The presentation was scheduled to start at four.

# Fourteen

Miss Perkins and Sam arrived at the tent to find Jim, the second member of Gaston's security team, busy behind the tiny bar, polishing glasses. Although he was half hidden behind a vast ice bucket holding two magnums of champagne, Sam could see that he was a substantial man, verging on huge, dressed in a black suit, and wearing pitch-black sunglasses. As he left the bar to greet them, Miss Perkins let out a cry of recognition.

*"Jim, c'est toi! Quelle bonne surprise!"*

Jim beamed, whipped off his sunglasses, and kissed Miss Perkins loudly on each cheek.

"I guess you two know each other," said Sam.

It was Miss Perkins's turn to beam. "Indeed we do, don't we, Jim? We've been going to the same cookery course all winter, and I must tell you that this young man makes the best cheese soufflé in Marseille." She kissed her fingertips. "Such a light touch." She bustled away and put the pile of bound presentation documents on the table. "There. Each of these has a committee member's name on. Or, as you would say, dear, personalized."

"How do you know their names?"

Miss Perkins looked at Sam as though he were a backward child. "I made inquiries at the project office. Now let's see. The project model is up at the far end, where everyone can see it. I suppose we have to put that ghastly chairman here, at the head of the table."

"You know him too?"

"I met him at the consulate many years ago, when he was a *very* junior dogsbody. A shifty little monkey, even then. Not to be trusted, dear, mark my words."

Jim had positioned himself at the entrance to welcome any early arrivals, and Sam made a final tour of the tent, which looked crisp, professional, and inviting under the golden glow of filtered sunlight. He felt a surge of hope. There would be opposition from Patrimonio, that was inevitable, but he was confident of finding a few open minds among the members of the committee. A pity Reboul couldn't be here.

Shortly after four o'clock the first members of the committee arrived, putting up the merest token resistance to a welcoming glass of champagne. By 4:15 all seven of them had been seated at their places around the table, each with his glass and his copy of the presentation document. The atmosphere quickly became relaxed.

The chairman's chair remained conspicuously empty for

another ten minutes, and Sam was considering a reward for patience in the form of a further distribution of champagne when there was a flurry at the entrance of the tent. It was Patrimonio, shooting his cuffs, smoothing his hair, and announcing that he had been delayed by a very important phone call. He was in black today—a silk suit—with a white shirt and a sober, blue-striped tie.

This immediately caught the attention of Miss Perkins. "I cannot believe he went to Eton," she whispered to Sam, "but that's an Old Etonian tie he's wearing." She sniffed. "The impertinence of the man."

With Patrimonio finally seated, the presentation could begin. Miss Perkins delivered a few words in her excellent French, explaining the purpose of the documents and instructing the committee members to raise their hands if Sam said anything they didn't understand.

As he began, Sam reminded himself of the advice he had been given by one of the old partners when working many years ago in corporate law. "Don't get complicated. Tell them what you're going to tell them. Tell them. Then tell them what you've told them."

He soon felt that he had a sympathetic audience, and he was right. The previous day they had endured the presentation of Madame Dumas and her team from Paris, who had bombarded the committee for several hours with forecasts, feasibility studies, estimates, cost analyses, charts, graphs, and occupancy predictions. Sam's presentation, helped no doubt by the occasional refill of champagne, was a complete contrast:

simple and easy to understand. Looking around the table, it appeared that some members of the committee had actually found it enjoyable.

With one exception. The chairman remained wooden-faced throughout Sam's performance, declining champagne, heaving the occasional sigh, and consulting his watch frequently. But he was the first to speak when Sam had finished and invited questions.

Rising to his feet and clearing his throat, Patrimonio launched into his remarks. "Land, as we all know, is very limited in Marseille, particularly land overlooking the sea. And yet here we have a proposition that ignores this basic fact. We find an extravagant amount of room being taken up by a nonessential garden and a marina of doubtful usefulness. This is bad enough. But even worse, by keeping the height of the buildings to only three stories, there is a waste of air space that I can only call reckless. Developments of this sort may be acceptable in America"—Patrimonio jerked his head toward Sam—"where there is almost unlimited land, but here we must be aware of the restrictions imposed by local resources. We can no longer afford horizontal expansion. The way forward is upward." He paused and nodded, as if pleased with his little *bon mot.* "Yes, the way forward is upward. I'm sure my colleagues will agree." And with that, he looked around the table, eyebrows raised, as he waited, if not for applause, then at least for support.

Sam broke an embarrassing silence by repeating the benefits of his scheme, principally that it would provide shelter and enjoyment for the people of Marseille rather than for tourists. This prompted several nods around the table.

Patrimonio scowled. "I hope you will excuse me. I have another meeting to attend. I will discuss this later with members of the committee."

With Patrimonio gone, the mood in the tent lightened. With another glass of champagne all around, it lightened even more, and it was nearly an hour before the last member of the committee drifted off.

Miss Perkins had spent that hour chatting to members of the committee. "Well, dear," she said, "you should be pleased. That went very well, except for the chairman's contribution. But I don't think you should let that worry you. From what I heard, he was definitely a lone voice. The comments made to me were extremely positive. Does Mr. Patrimonio have a great deal of influence?"

"We'll see," said Sam. "It's a difficult one to call. I'm sure he's going to twist a few arms."

Miss Perkins patted his hand. "Don't you worry, dear. He's not very well liked, you know. One can tell from the odd word dropped here and there. We must relax, and let hope spring eternal."


*The Floating Pound,* taking up two berths, was moored stern first against the quay in Saint-Tropez, where passers-by could admire the opulence of the afterdeck and watch—at a distance, of course—the start of the cocktail hour on board.

Annabel had spent much of the short voyage from Marseille on the phone, organizing an impromptu cocktail party, and had managed to round up a mixed bag of expatriates and vacationers. These could be identified by their complexions: brown and leathery for the expats; varying degrees of pink, from blush to medium-rare, for the visitors. They shared a fondness for white clothes and conspicuous gold jewelry, and an observer could be forgiven for thinking that they were members of the chorus in a summer variety show.

"Darling!" "Sweetie!" "It's been *ages!*" "You look *fabulous!* The Botox really worked!" "Divine!" "Mmmm!" And so it went on—the sound track of summer in Saint-Trop.

Lord Wapping, his good humor restored by a long, champagne-induced nap, had gone through his wardrobe in search of something appropriate for the occasion. He had finally chosen a billowing caftan in white (with gold brocade highlights) which, if you believed Annabel, made him look like a Roman emperor in his Sunday-best toga. He moved among his guests, stately and tentlike, and was beginning to forget his cares and enjoy himself when he heard, coming from the inner billows of his caftan, the sound of his cell phone.

It was Patrimonio, an agitated Patrimonio, with disturbing news. Following that afternoon's presentation, he had made brief calls to the members of his committee. Almost to a man, they had been extremely enthusiastic about what they had heard, and Patrimonio had the distinct feeling that some of them had already made up their minds in favor of Sam's proposal.

"Shit!" Wapping's guests stopped in midgossip, and he moved out of earshot. "I thought you said you had them in your pocket."

"There is still your presentation to come, don't forget. If there is something special you could offer . . ."

Wapping's special offers were usually limited to bribery or coercion, but he could see that brute force could hardly be used on all seven committee members. "What's it going to cost to make them change their minds?"

There was a moment of silence while Patrimonio considered the possibility of wholesale bribery. "It's very delicate," he said at last. "Even supposing they all accepted, if it ever got out, if the mayor got to hear about it . . . No, I don't think we dare to try that."

"Fat lot of help you are. Use your head, man—there must be something that would put him out of the running."

Patrimonio sighed. "Well, of course if the American could be persuaded to withdraw his bid, we would be in a much stronger position."

Wapping left his guests to their own noisy devices and found a quiet corner on the upper deck. He needed to think.

Reboul listened to Sam's account of the presentation with considerable satisfaction. "So that little nonsense about land being scarce was all Patrimonio said? No interruptions? No comments as you were going through the details? Well, it sounds as though it could hardly have gone better. Congratulations, my friend, but also a word of warning: Patrimonio and Wapping—it's a dangerous combination, and they're not going to give in without a fight. Don't let your guard drop. But enough of that. You must celebrate this afternoon's success, and take the delightful Mademoiselle Elena out to dinner."

They left Mimi in charge of Philippe and, following his advice, made their way to Chez Marco, a bistro tucked away behind the Vieux Port. Pausing at the entrance, they looked in vain for a menu. Marco served *steack* with *frites*, or *steack* without *frites*, with the option of a salad. And that was it. Despite this, almost every table was taken, the ambiance was loud and friendly, and their waiter fell in love with them at the first sound of Sam's accent. He adored Americans, he told them, having spent three months working in a restaurant in downtown New York, where he had been amazed—*époustouflé!*—by the generosity of his tips. He took their order and brought them a carafe of red wine.

It was soft and round and surprisingly good. The steaks were juicy and perfectly cooked, and the *frites* were a connoisseur's delight. But the real triumph, according to Elena, came with the salad. "You can always tell a good restaurant by its dressing," she said, "and this is terrific. They've used just the right amount of balsamic vinegar."

Sam realized that, thanks to Philippe, they had stumbled upon a minor treasure—a restaurant that was content to provide a very limited choice, but of the highest quality, and at old-fashioned prices. According to Philippe, there used to be simple little restaurants like this throughout France; now they had become few and far between, killed off by the invasion of fast-food chains. But Chez Marco, it seemed, was doing fine.

A knot of customers waited at the battered zinc bar, and tables were taken as soon as they became free. The laughter level was high, the waiters agile, and behind the bar the *patron*, Marco himself, dispensed pastis, jokes, and insults with a broad gap-toothed smile.

Elena used her bread to wipe the last of the dressing from her plate. "Apart from the food, you know what's so great about this place? It's genuine. Nobody designed it. A decorator would have a heart attack, but it works. Do you think they do dessert?"

They did. Again, the choice was limited to one. *Panna cotta*, made by Marco's Italian wife and served in a thick glass tumbler, a white, satiny mixture of heavy cream and vanilla with a dense topping of semi-liquid caramel. Elena took her first spoonful and sighed with pleasure. "Heaven."

# *Fifteen*

The Mediterranean was a sheet of black glass—flat, calm, with a sickle moon high in a clear sky, as *The Floating Pound* eased slowly out of Saint-Tropez and turned west, destination Marseille.

Lord Wapping felt that he needed to get back to oversee the execution of an idea that was beginning to take shape in his head, and there was not a moment to lose. Hurried farewells had been made to his guests, and they had been hustled down the gangway, much to the displeasure of Annabel, who had no desire to leave Saint-Tropez, which she considered her spiritual summer home.

"I'm absolutely *devastated,* sweetie," she said, displaying once again her ability to pout and talk at the same time. "The Forsyths—you know, Fiona and Dickie—had booked a table at the Byblos for dinner, and then we were going dancing. And now this. It's too, too boring. Do we *have* to go back?"

Wapping grunted. "Something's come up." He added an invaluable phrase, knowing that it would put an end to any argument. "It's business." Experience had taught him that in Annabel's mind business was synonymous with Cartier, Dior, Vuitton, and all the other little essentials of life that came her way after a successful deal. And so, for her, everything else took second place to business. Off she went, to find sympathy and a consoling glass of champagne with Tiny de Salis, while Wapping settled down in the deserted stateroom to ponder.

The presentation of his project was about to take place. A successful result would get the banks off his back and put millions into his pocket. The Parisian presentation, enthusiastically sabotaged by Patrimonio, had not impressed the committee. But that left the problem of the American. Patrimonio's words came back to him: "If he could be persuaded to withdraw, that would put us in a much stronger position."

Of course it would. But how? He considered once again those two old favorites, bribery and violence, and once again rejected them. The American stood to make more money out of the project than any bribe Wapping was able to offer, and any force short of murder was unlikely to work. In any case, to be credible and effective the withdrawal had to be voluntary; it had to come from the American himself. Lord Wapping stared out of the porthole, sipping the last of his 1936 cognac and letting his mind go back to the idea that had come to him, half-formed, following Patrimonio's call. The more he thought about it, the better it seemed. And by the time he finally braved the chilly reception that awaited him in the cabin he shared with Annabel, he was feeling a great deal more optimistic.

The following morning, back at her old Marseille mooring in the Baie du Grand Soufre, *The Floating Pound* had recovered her good humor and was once again a happy ship. Lord Wapping was positively jovial at breakfast. Annabel had been tempted out of her sulk by the promise of an all-expenses-paid swoop on Marseille's best boutiques, followed by lunch at Peron. Ray Prendergast had celebrated the change in the atmosphere on board with a solid English breakfast of sausages, bacon, eggs, baked beans, and two thick, greasy slices of fried bread. And the crew, having been a little disappointed by their brief glimpse of the prosperous respectability of Saint-Tropez, were pleased to be back in Marseille, with its superior opportunities for bad behavior.

Lord Wapping was humming the opening bars of "My Old Man's a Dustman" as he selected his first cigar of the day. He was in the positive, benign mood that often follows the solution of a difficult problem, and he called Ray Prendergast into the stateroom to share his thoughts.

"I think I've cracked it, Ray—that bloody American and his beach huts. Somehow we've got to put him out of the running, and I think I've got the answer. Here's what we're going to do."

As he explained his idea, Prendergast's expression gradually changed from alarm to doubt to qualified approval. "It's a bit dodgy, Billy, but it could work. I'll have a chat with Brian and Dave. It's a question of opportunity, isn't it? Finding the right moment. But first, we need to know where he's living. Oh, and another thing: We're going to need a doctor, a friendly doctor. Know what I mean?"

Wapping nodded. "Leave it to me." With a wave of his cigar, he dismissed Prendergast before reaching for the phone.

"Jérôme? Couple of questions for you. I've been thinking about our little problem, and I need to know where our American friend is living while he's in Marseille. Have you got his address?"

"Certainly." Patrimonio reached into a drawer of his desk and pulled out a folder. "All the bidders had to provide contact details when they registered. Let's see. Ah, yes, here it is: the Chemin du Roucas Blanc. Do you want the full address and the phone number?"

Patrimonio's curiosity got the better of him while Wapping was jotting down the details. "What do you have in mind?"

"Oh, a bit of this, a bit of that, a bit of the other. Here's the second question: I need a tame doctor—you know, someone who does what you want with no questions. That kind of doctor."

As it happened, Patrimonio had several times needed just such a doctor himself, to help him deal with the results of some ill-advised liaisons with young ladies. He cleared his throat. "I might be able to help you there. What will you expect him to do, this doctor?"

"Jérôme, you don't want to know."

"Of course not. No. Well, someone I can recommend is Doctor Hoffmann. German, but very good, very discreet, very—how can I put it?—very cooperative. And she speaks excellent English."

"She?"

"Oh yes. But don't worry—she can do anything a man can do. Would you like me to call her?"

Wapping was smiling as he put the phone down. The day was turning out better than he expected.

With the presentation over and all the committee members' supplementary questions dealt with, there was nothing for Elena and Sam to do except keep their fingers crossed and wait for the decision. And so they had decided to take a break and look around the *arrière-pays*—the back country behind and to the west of Marseille.

They explored Provence's most fashionable mountain ranges, the Luberon and the Alpilles, where, so it was said, movie stars, eminent politicians, and lesser celebrities haunted the hill villages and lurked behind every high stone wall. They saw the pink flamingos of the Camargue, the vast emptiness of Haute-Provence, the seething village markets, and the massed ranks of antique dealers in L'Isle-sur-Sorgue. As they went, they tasted the wines of Provence, sometimes in garages, sometimes in eighteenth-century palaces—the chilled sweetness of Beaumes de Venise, the big, voluptuous reds of Châteauneuf-du-Pape, the noble *rosés* of Tavel.

And they ate, always well and sometimes memorably. Philippe had sent them off with a list of his favorite addresses, and they quickly slipped into the French habit of planning the day's sightseeing around the stomach. Thus, lunchtime and the dinner hour would conveniently find them close to a little *auberge* or an exceptional chef.

Not surprisingly, all thoughts of presentations and projects were forgotten in the leisurely, magical haze of sunshine and shared discovery. Time seemed to have stopped. Elena was in a state of bliss, and Sam wasn't far behind.

Meanwhile, a million miles away in Marseille, Lord Wapping was making his formal proposal to the committee. To help him—in fact, to make the presentation on his behalf—he had employed Frédéric Millet, a young man with impeccable credentials, being not only bilingual but also a cousin of Jérôme Patrimonio, whose taste in clothes and aftershave he had adopted.

As Frédéric went through his charts and explanations, it became clear that at least two members of his audience were firmly on his side. Wapping and Patrimonio, nodding in unison at the appearance of each chart, accompanied the proceedings from time to time with murmured sounds of approval. *"Bravo, bonne idée"* and *"très bien"* coming from Patrimonio, and "nice work, Fred" or "you tell 'em, sunshine" from Wapping, who was feeling increasingly confident.

Frédéric had barely finished when Patrimonio got to his feet to deliver the chairman's summing-up of what they had just heard. After the obligatory cuff-shooting and hair-smoothing, he plunged in. "First, let me congratulate Lord Wapping and his colleague Monsieur Millet on a most interesting and comprehensive presentation." The brief niceties over, the Patrimonio brow furrowed, and his face took on the sincere, serious, deeply caring expression of a salesman about to pounce. "This scheme, it seems to me, fulfills all of our requirements. From the architectural point of view, it is very much of today, and I can see that before long it will have established itself as a contemporary landmark—a building with aesthetic resonance that will add enormously to the prestige of the Marseille coastline. Next, as you have heard, the scheme will generate hundreds of new jobs, not just during the period of construction, but permanently, for the operation and maintenance of all the facilities that have been described to us. It is difficult to predict in detail the benefits this will bring to the local economy, but it is safe to say that they will be very, very substantial. And finally, let me add a comment about a matter which, as you know, I consider to be most important—you might say it is the bee in the chairman's bonnet." He paused, as if to allow the committee to picture the chairman in his bonnet. "Air space, gentlemen. Air space. A precious resource, so often neglected. But here we see it maximized as it should be. I have no hesitation in commending this scheme to the members of the committee."

Later, in the bar of the Sofitel, Wapping and Patrimonio compared impressions.

"Pretty glum lot, your committee," said Wapping. "Not much in the way of questions. What do you reckon they thought of it?"

Patrimonio took a pensive sip of his whisky. "You must remember that these people make their living by sitting on the fence. We must wait and see. These things always take a little while to sink in. But we have ten days before the final decision will be made, and I shall use the time to do some lobbying—a lunch or two, a glass of champagne after work . . ." Patrimonio waved a generous hand to suggest the irresistible range of inducements available to a man of his position.

Wapping said nothing. He was too busy thinking about his own lobbying.

Ray Prendergast made his way up the Rue de Rome until he came to a low white building set back from the street. One of the brass plaques next to the entrance, more highly polished than the others, had the name of Dr. Romy Hoffmann engraved on it in fine copperplate script. Prendergast pressed the bell and the door clicked open.

Dr. Hoffmann's assistant, a burly man in a white track suit, his head shaved and gleaming, showed Prendergast into an empty, all-white waiting room, where elderly copies of *Stern* magazine shared a low table with *Paris Match* and *Gala*. A TV set in one corner was showing a promotional film made by a pharmaceutical company in which two young women were having an animated conversation about menopause.

Prendergast looked at his watch. He had made the mistake of arriving on time for the appointment, forgetting that punctuality is the sworn enemy of the medical profession. He had been waiting for twenty minutes when a metallic voice emanating from a speaker in the corner told him that he should come through.

Dr. Hoffmann, a small, wiry woman in her forties, was

dressed in a white cotton top and trousers, a surgical facemask hanging round her neck. Her dark hair was cropped short, her eyes concealed by tinted glasses. She gestured toward the chair in front of her desk. "Please. Sit. Monsieur Patrimonio told me to expect you. Tell me what brings you here."

Ray Prendergast took a deep breath and started to talk.

For Brian and Dave, this was, as Lord Wapping had made clear, a last chance to redeem themselves. Their encounter with the journalist had been partly successful, although not successful enough to stop him making a bloody pest of himself after the accident. As for the business of the tent on the beach, the less said about that the better. They had, in their employer's words, made a right Horlicks of it.

This time, they were to make no mistakes. But as they had agreed after the briefing from Prendergast, this was their kind of job: a bit of detective work, some shadowing, and just a touch of the nasty at the end. No worries. They rented a nondescript Peugeot, bought a street map of Marseille, and set off one morning for the Chemin du Roucas Blanc, parking a comfortable distance away from the gated entrance.

With painful slowness, the hours went by. People came and went, but not the people they were interested in. The Peugeot, despite its place in the shade of a tree, became intolerably hot. Dave nearly got himself arrested when a resident saw him responding to a pressing call of nature up against a garden wall.

They quickly learned to recognize those who came and

went on a regular basis: Nanou the maid on her Mobylette, Claudine the housekeeper in her Fiat 500, Olivier the chauffeur in the big black car—sometimes with passengers, sometimes without. But not once did they see the solitary figure they were hoping to see. Tedious hours turned into tedious days, broken up by shadowing Olivier from time to time as he went off to carry out some errand in the city.

Their patience was finally rewarded one bright afternoon by the arrival of a taxi that roused Dave from his afternoon doze by sounding its horn at the gate.

"It's empty," said Brian. "Come to pick someone up."

Dave focused his binoculars on the gate a hundred yards away, saw the taxi appear and pull out onto the road with a single female passenger in the back. "Right," he said. "Let's go."

At a safe distance, they followed the taxi back down the winding Chemin du Roucas Blanc, closing the gap when the traffic thickened as they reached the center of town. They went along the side of the Vieux Port, through a narrow side street, and emerged into the Rue Paradis. The taxi came to a halt outside a tinted glass façade, and they saw Elena Morales get out and go through the entrance marked "Studio Céline Coiffure."

"Gone for a hairdo, it looks like," said Dave. "This could do us nicely if we can find somewhere to park."

After ten minutes of automotive infighting, Brian managed to shoehorn the Peugeot into a spot opposite the salon, provoking a barrage of shouts and horn-blowing from frustrated drivers backed up behind him. A young man in a battered Renault extended his hand in the classic single-digit salute as he passed. "And the same to you, mate," said Brian. "No bleeding manners, these French."

"Not long now," said Dave. "Got your syringe?"

Brian nodded. "Got yours?"

They waited a few minutes more, then left the car, crossed the street, and appeared to find something that fascinated them in the window of a menswear boutique two doors away from the salon.

Elena came out into the bright sunshine of the street and was putting on her sunglasses when Brian, holding a map, went up to her. "Excuse me, miss," he said. "Do you speak any English?"

"Sure."

"I'm a bit lost." He moved around to be beside her, holding the map so that she could see it. Dave came up behind her and jabbed the needle of his syringe into the bicep of her bare arm. The effect was instant. Her head slumped forward, her legs started to give way. They had to stop her from collapsing and almost had to carry her across the street before putting her into the back seat of the Peugeot. Passers-by took one look and hurried on. In Marseille one didn't interfere in such situations.

Brian was grinning as he started the engine. "Works a treat, that stuff, doesn't it?"

Sam checked his watch. Six-thirty, that time of day when stomachs all over Marseille start to rumble in anticipation. He and Elena had arranged to have dinner with Mimi and Philippe, but where was she? How long could a haircut take? Or had shopping caused her to lose track of the time?

He called her cell phone, but there was no answer. He called again twenty minutes later, and again ten minutes after that. Still no answer. By 7:30 he was worried enough to call Reboul. An hour later, Reboul called back. "My people have checked with the police, and with the hospitals and clinics. There have been no reports of any accidents or emergencies involving anyone of Elena's description. I'm very sorry, my friend, but so far we've drawn a blank. We'll keep trying."

Sam passed a miserable evening with Philippe and Mimi. They made more unsuccessful calls to Elena's number. Philippe called all his contacts—the informers, the night people, bar and club owners, a friend who owned a private ambulance service. Nothing. Evening stretched into what would prove to be a long, black, sleepless night for Sam.

Tired of pacing the bedroom, and more in desperation than hope, he tried Elena's number. This time there was an answer.

"We were hoping you'd call." The voice at the other end sounded tinny and slightly distorted, as if speaking through some kind of baffle, but it was distinct enough.

Sam made an effort to stay calm. "Where's Elena?"

"Oh, she's fine."

"Let me speak to her."

"That won't be possible, I'm afraid. She's catching up on her sleep. It would be a shame to disturb her."

"Where is she? Who are you?"

"That needn't concern you. Now listen carefully. Miss Morales will be returned to you unharmed as soon as you withdraw your bid for the development on the Anse des Pêcheurs, officially and unconditionally. You may give any excuse you want—apart, of course, from the real one. Is that clear? You can call me on this number when you've made the necessary arrangements. I'd advise you not to waste any time."

"How do I know you'll keep your word?"

"You don't."

"Why should I believe you?"

"What other options do you have?"

There was a click, and the line went dead.

# Sixteen

Philippe was already in the kitchen, standing at the window and nursing his first espresso, when Sam came in—a haggard, unshaven, red-eyed Sam wearing his rumpled clothes from the day before and clutching his cell phone. He got himself a cup of coffee and sat down.

"Still no news?" asked Philippe. Sam shook his head. The night before, when Sam had told him about the phone call, Philippe had once again called the police, the hospitals, his underworld contacts, and the emergency services. As before, the result had been a series of blanks. It was time to acknowledge the ugly fact that last night's caller had been serious; Elena had been kidnapped.

Philippe came and sat down. He put his arm around Sam's shoulder, wincing as his cracked ribs complained. "I know it's hard, but let's try to be logical about this. *D'accord?*" Sam sighed and nodded. Philippe continued: "It's not a normal ransom job, because nobody's asked you for money. They've been very specific about what they want and how they want it done. Also, the guy spoke in English. Did he have any kind of accent?"

"Hard to tell. His voice was distorted."

"That's standard procedure." Philippe shook his head. "*Putain*—I'm starting to talk like a cop. But did he sound English, or like a Frenchman speaking English?"

Despite the distortion, Sam remembered, the voice had sounded completely at home with English. "Now that I think about it, I'm pretty sure he was English. A Frenchman nearly always has difficulty pronouncing English words that begin with an *h*. This guy didn't have a problem."

"Right. So an Englishman calls you and wants you to pull out of the project. Now who's going to do that? Who would gain from it? Who else could it be but Wapping or one of his entourage?" Philippe got up to make some more coffee. "It has to be him." He looked at Sam and shrugged. "That's the easy part. Now we have to work out where he's holding Elena. Bear in mind that he doesn't know Marseille very well, so he's not going to hide her in some apartment. I'm pretty sure he wouldn't involve Patrimonio in something like this. That would make Patrimonio an accomplice to a criminal act—too risky. Now put yourself in Wapping's shoes. He needs to keep Elena somewhere secure, somewhere discreet, somewhere he has total control. Where does that lead us?"

"The boat?"

"Exactly. *The Floating Pound*, where there's no chance of any outsiders seeing something they shouldn't. Also, if he has a problem he can just sail away. Plus, he has the helicopter. So let's assume that we know who the kidnapper is, and we know where he's keeping Elena. Now we come to the hard part. Somehow, we have to get onto the boat."

"Philippe, just a minute. Where are the police in all this? Why can't we get them to raid the boat?"

Philippe shook his head slowly, and took a deep breath. "Down here, we don't like getting on the wrong side of rich foreigners. It's bad for business. Marseille has had enough trouble with its reputation already. But more important, much more important, there isn't any evidence—no recording of that phone call, no witnesses, no clues. Just our little theory, our word, that's all. No proof. And without something to go on, no cop is going to board a private vessel."

"Don't you have a really solid police contact we could talk to? An inspector?"

"Andreis? He retired—went off to Corsica to make cheese."

Sam had started the morning feeling desperately worried and frustrated. Now he was getting angry. The thought of Elena being used as a bargaining chip made him crave action, preferably something that involved breaking Wapping's neck. And with the anger came a rush of energy, all memories of a sleepless night forgotten.

"OK, so we need to search that boat. If we can't use the police, then we have to think of something that will make the search look official. Otherwise they won't even let us on board."

Sam's phone rang. He grabbed at it, nerves making him clumsy. It was Reboul, hoping in vain for good news. He was shocked to hear about the kidnap call. "Sam, I don't know what to say. It's my fault for getting you into this mess. I just want you to know that you can count on me for any help I can give you. Anything at all. What are you going to do?"

"I'm working on it. I'll let you know."

While he'd been on the phone, a tousled, yawning Mimi had joined them. She went over to Sam and put her arms round him. "Still nothing?"

Sam shook his head and bent down to kiss her forehead. It was burning hot. "Mimi, are you feeling all right? You've got a hell of a temperature."

"Oh, it's nothing serious. There's some bug going around. I'll be fine."

There are times when the mind makes some curious random connections, and Mimi's bug took Sam back to an unhealthy moment in Marseille's history. "You two would know more about it than me, but wasn't there a big plague in Marseille back in the eighteenth century? I remember reading about it."

Philippe looked puzzled. "It was in 1720," he said. "When they weren't bothering too much with quarantine. Thousands of people died."

"So I guess there must now be quarantine restrictions."

"Of course. Especially now, you know, given all the problems with illegal immigration. Why do you ask?"

"Well, suppose there was a report that some contagious disease might have been brought into Marseille on a boat—let's say, a boat from the Ivory Coast. Wouldn't the quarantine authorities want to do some emergency health checks, to make sure it wasn't spreading?"

For the first time that morning, Philippe grinned. "I think I can see what's coming."

"A team from Health and Immigration, with a couple of cops as official backup, to inspect all foreign-registry boats."

"Starting with Wapping's boat?"

"Exactly. But at night, when nobody's expecting a visit."

In ten minutes, they had worked out a shopping list, and Sam called Reboul.

"Francis, we have an idea, but to make it work we need a police speedboat, two guys who could pass as police officers, and a few medical accessories. For tonight. Can you help?"

Reboul took a moment to think. "The speedboat is no problem. Nor is the medical equipment. The police officers—ah, yes, I think I know just the men for that. Give me half an hour to set things up, and meet me in an hour at the private terminal at Marignane. Bring your passport just in case. You can tell me all about your idea while we're on our way."

"Where are we going?"

"Corsica, my friend. Corsica."

Sam was shaking his head as he put down the phone. "How simple life is when you're a billionaire. It looks like we're all set."

Philippe had been pacing up and down in an agony of curiosity. "Well? Well?"

"Reboul is taking me to Corsica this morning. I think we're going to have a meeting with two fake cops." Sam went over to Mimi, who curled up in an armchair. He kissed her burning forehead once more for luck. "I'll never forget you gave me the idea. Now take a couple of aspirin and get back to bed."

When Sam arrived at Marignane's private air terminal, Reboul was already waiting, his cell phone to his ear. He finished his call and came over to embrace Sam. "I'm so sorry about this. So very sorry."

In fact, Sam was feeling better and more positive than he'd felt for several hours. He was no longer passive, just waiting; he was doing something, and activity is a sovereign remedy for most problems. He clapped Reboul on the shoulder. "This is going to work. I know it's going to work once we find our cops."

"You'll see," said Reboul. "Let's get on the plane and I'll tell you about them."

Once again, Sam was struck by the boarding process, or rather by the lack of it, when flying private. They strolled across the tarmac to the plane, where the copilot welcomed them at the top of the gangway. The steps were retracted, the pilot taxied over to the takeoff point, and they began the short hop to Calvi, on the west coast of Corsica. Boarding time: three minutes.

Coffee was served by the copilot, and Reboul began his briefing. He started with the names of the two gentlemen they were going to meet: the Figatelli brothers, Florian and Joseph, known as Flo and Jo. Reboul had known them since the two were boys, when their father ran a hotel in which Reboul had a majority interest. When the father died after a hunting accident, Reboul had taken the two young men under his wing, offering to put them through university. To their mother's dismay and with Reboul's wholehearted approval, they had chosen to complete their education in Las Vegas, where a small but select college offered a course in celebrity hotel management.

English, naturally, was part of the curriculum. There was also detailed instruction on the running of a hotel, even down to the pitfalls of hiring illegal immigrants, the importance of clean fingernails, the art of increasing the tip, and, not least of all, the defensive measures to be taken if a distinguished guest, such as a United States senator, should be discovered *in flagrante* with a couple of the local hookers.

Flo and Jo graduated with honors, and to mark the occasion they were each presented with a special T-shirt, of black silk, with the city's motto embroidered in tasteful gold lettering: "What Happens in Vegas Stays in Vegas." Ready for the real world, they returned to Calvi and took over the management of the hotel. They ran it well, and they expanded their business to include bars, a beach franchise, and one or two enterprises that were not, strictly speaking, legal.

"But they're good boys," said Reboul, "and I trust them to do a good job."

"They need to look official, Francis. What about uniforms?"

Reboul tapped the side of his nose. "They already have regulation police uniforms. I can't think why. Better not to ask."

The plane was beginning its descent toward Calvi when Reboul leaned forward. "One thing we haven't talked about,

Sam. You mentioned a doctor. Where are we going to find our doctor?"

"You're looking at him."

"You? You can't go. They've met you. They know you."

"Not with a surgical mask, a pair of glasses, hospital scrubs, and one of those little hats they wear in the operating room. All they'll see of me is my eyebrows."

Reboul rubbed his chin in thought. "Well, maybe. But they'll recognize your voice, your accent."

"I won't speak English. In fact, I won't speak to them at all. I won't need to. I'll have my secret weapon."

"What's that?"

"A bilingual nurse."

Calvi, according to legend the birthplace of Christopher Columbus, is one of the most beautiful sights in an island filled with beautiful sights. The six-hundred-year-old citadel, built on a promontory, dominates a town of sweeping sea views and narrow streets, and it was in a bar in one of these narrow streets that Sam and Reboul met the Figatellis.

The Pourquoi Pas looked like dozens of other Mediterranean bars: fishing nets, soccer posters, a framed and autographed snapshot of Johnny Hallyday, a flat-screen TV, and several fine old mirrors with the gray bloom of the years visible through the glass. It had been chosen for the meeting because it belonged to the Figatellis, and it had a very private back room.

"You're a little early," said the girl behind the bar. "They're on their way. Please follow me." She led them into a small room stacked with cases of pastis and Corsican whisky. A wooden table with four chairs had been set up in the middle of the room and, while they settled down, the girl came back with a tray—two coffees, two shot glasses, and a plain dark-green bottle with a handwritten label that simply said "Flo & Jo."

Reboul noticed Sam looking at it. "That's *myrte*," he said, "the Corsican liqueur made with aromatic myrtle. Some people call it the fisherman's breakfast." He filled the glasses and handed one to Sam. "Here's to Elena, and her quick return."

Sam took a sip. It was thick and honey-sweet, with a powerful, slightly astringent kick that went all the way down. "That's good. Homemade?"

Reboul was just starting to explain the mysteries of making *myrte* when the door opened and the Figatelli brothers appeared, each carrying a bulging bag. They descended on Reboul with terrifying enthusiasm, kissing him, patting him, squeezing him. "Eh, Sissou, it's good to see you. Where have you been all this time? What's going on? Who's your friend?"

Introductions were made, and Sam's hand was vigorously mauled by each of them. Brawny, barrel-chested, black-haired, with the blue eyes that one sometimes finds around the Mediterranean, they looked tough and competent. "Serious men" was how Reboul had described them. He looked at his watch. "We don't have much time. Did you bring the uniforms?" The Figatellis nodded. "Good. Now let me fill you in."

Half an hour later, the four of them were on their way back to the airport. Sam had been impressed by the way the brothers had responded to the briefing, listening intently, interrupting only to ask intelligent questions. He allowed himself to feel renewed stirrings of optimism. Now all he had to do was recruit his nurse.

He called her from the plane. "Daphne, it's Sam. I've got a real problem. Could you possibly meet me at the house in an hour or so?"

"What have you been up to, you naughty boy? Of course I'll be there." As Daphne Perkins finished the call she experienced an agreeable tingle of anticipation. She had arranged an afternoon of whist and polite conversation with some friends, but this would undoubtedly be more interesting. Sam was always getting up to something interesting. Such a scamp.

Elena stirred, opened her eyes, and tried to sit up. She felt thick and nauseous. Her throat was dry, and she was having difficulty focusing. She was barely aware of the figure sitting at her side in the darkened cabin, barely felt the needle going into her arm. She slept again.

"If you have a bottle of stout, dear, that would do very nicely. It's the heat."

Sam looked in the fridge. The nearest thing to stout he could find was a bottle of German *Bock*, which he poured into a glass and put in front of Daphne. She took a long, thirsty swallow. "That's *much* better, dear. Thank you. Those roads are so hot, and my poor old 2CV doesn't have air-conditioning." She took another swallow, and dabbed her lips with a lace hand-kerchief. "Now then. What is this problem you mentioned?"

By the time Sam had finished explaining, Daphne's mouth was tight with anger. "Blackguards!" she said. "They should be horsewhipped. That poor, poor girl. What can I do to help?"

Sam took her through the preparations that were being made for the rescue attempt. "And I'm going to be the doctor," he said. "But here's the problem. I can disguise my appearance, but I can't disguise my voice. So I'm going to pretend to be a French doctor who doesn't speak a word of English. And that's where I hope you come in, as an interpreter with full medical qualifications, able to pass on my instructions in English. In other words, you will be Nurse Perkins, the doctor's right arm." Sam looked at her, his expression quizzical, his head cocked. "That is, if you're prepared to do it."

The beam on Daphne's face was answer enough. "What fun!" she said. "Of course I'll do it."

"You don't happen to have a nurse's uniform, by any chance?"

Daphne pursed her lips. "It's been many years since a man asked me that, dear. I don't. But I can get one from my friend who works at La Timone. It's a big hospital, and they have everything there—plenty of uniforms. Shall I get a stetho-scope as well?"

Sam was smiling with relief. "Why not? Actually, get two."

They agreed that Daphne should come back to the house that evening around nine o'clock, and they would set off for the

Vieux Port just before ten. As Sam watched her drive the old Deux Chevaux through the gate, he gave her a mental three cheers. With women like that, he thought, it was no wonder the British Empire had lasted so long.

Sam found Mimi and Philippe by the pool—Mimi wrapped up on a *chaise longue* under a parasol, and Philippe in the shallow end doing the exercises that had been prescribed by his nurse. He waved to Sam and climbed up the steps from the pool, wincing as he climbed. "It's bizarre," he said, "I can move in the water with no pain at all, but now . . . *ouf!* How did you get on?"

"We have our nurse: Miss Perkins, the lady who helped me out with the presentation. She's terrific. She'll be here tonight in her full nurse's regalia. If you like, I'll get her to take Mimi's temperature."

"What about your outfit?"

"Olivier's picking it up now. And the two boys from Corsica are coming up to the house at nine. We'll all go off together. If we get to the boat just after ten, between dinner and bedtime, that should be about right. With any luck they'll all be drunk."

"Is there room for a disabled journalist on the speedboat?"

"Not a chance. But look at it this way: you get the story without getting wet."

# Seventeen

A soft, warm Marseille evening held the promise of a fine, calm night. A good omen, Sam thought. You can plan just about everything else, but you can't plan the weather. Rain and a tearing mistral in an open speedboat would have made a depressing start to the expedition, and it was an expedition that had enough problems already.

He looked at his watch: 8:30. It was time to transform himself into Dr. Ginoux, specialist in contagious tropical diseases. He went into the bedroom, where his disguise—compliments of Reboul's contacts—had been laid out on the bed: a full set of hospital scrubs, a pair of white rubber Crocs (the discerning doctor's footwear of choice), a close-fitting cotton operating hat, a face mask, and a well-worn Gladstone bag. Next to these were two purchases Sam had made that afternoon: a high-tech light meter of the kind used by professional photographers, and a pair of heavy, black-framed glasses with plain lenses.

Sam took off his clothes. Was the correctly dressed doctor supposed to have medically approved underwear? Too bad. He put on the scrubs, the mask, the glasses, and the close-fitting hat, and went over to inspect himself in a full-length mirror, his Crocs squeaking on the parquet. A totally unrecognizable figure peered back at him. He felt a shiver of adrenaline. It wouldn't be long now.

He checked the contents in both sides of the Gladstone bag. There were enough thermometers to take the temperature of an entire boat's crew, several pairs of Latex gloves, a flashlight, spare face masks, and half a dozen loaded syringes. In the bag's other compartment, a selection of dressings, antiseptic ointment, and a stethoscope. He was ready. Now all he needed to do was to find the patient.

Mimi and Philippe, waiting for him in the living room, looked him over. Mimi pronounced Sam completely anonymous. And, she added, a little frightening.

Philippe did a tour of inspection around him, nodding as he went. "Very good," he said. "Maybe you could have a look at my ribs? No, seriously—not even Elena would recognize you."

Sam pushed the face mask down until it hung around his neck, took off the glasses and the hat, and looked at his watch. The hands seemed to be stuck.

"Waiting is hard, isn't it?" said Mimi.

"Sure is."

They heard the sound of tires on gravel and the slamming of car doors. Sam went to open the front door. The Figatelli brothers, still carrying their bulky bags, loomed large in the half-light of the entrance.

"You *en forme*, Sam? Ready to go? We've been down in the Vieux Port, checking the boat. Everything's fine, and we're lucky with the weather. The sea is like this." Jo passed a flat hand, palm down, in front of his body, as if stroking a straight line.

Sam introduced the brothers to Mimi and Philippe and had just shown them into the bedroom to change when he heard the tinny clatter of another car, Miss Perkins's 2CV. The final member of the team had arrived.

Nurse Perkins, as Sam would henceforth think of her, was an immaculate credit to the medical profession. A severe bun had replaced her normal, more relaxed hairstyle. Her long white jacket, starched rigid, carried a small battery of thermometers in one breast pocket. Pinned to the outside of the other pocket was a nurse's watch attached to a black ribbon. A starched white skirt, white stockings, white shoes, and a clipboard with pen completed the outfit. Florence Nightingale would have been proud of her.

"Perfect," said Sam. "Absolutely perfect."

"I do hope so, dear. I'm a little late because I had to restarch everything. These young girls nowadays never use enough, and then one becomes rumpled, which would never do for me."

Mimi and Philippe were watching, fascinated by this vision in white.

"Mimi and Philippe," said Sam, "meet Daphne. She's our secret weapon." Smiles and handshakes were exchanged, and Philippe was just about to ask exactly what a secret weapon would do on a boat when Daphne, looking over his shoulder, said, "Oh my goodness—what strapping young men."

With the change into police uniform, Flo and Jo seemed to have grown even bigger, the pistols and handcuffs on their belts adding an extra touch of menace to their already forbidding appearance. They saluted, took off their peaked hats, and grinned.

"Florian and Joseph," said Sam, "but I think they prefer to be called Flo and Jo."

"So much more chummy," said Daphne, looking from one to the other. "But how do we tell who's who?"

"I'm the good-looking one," they said in unison.

Sam led them through to the dining room and sat them down. "I'd like to go through a few points so we're all on the same page tonight. Stop me if you have any questions, OK?" He looked around at the attentive faces and smiled. "First, thank you for helping me. This is a lousy situation, and I don't know what I'd have done without you. These people have already gone after our friend here"—he nodded toward Philippe—"and when I think of them taking Elena, I feel . . . well, I'm sure you know how I feel. So thank you. Thank you very much."

Sam stopped to take a breath and gather his thoughts. "Now, problem number one is getting on board Wapping's boat. The uniforms are going to help, obviously, and then there's the cover story of a rogue virus going around the port. I'm hoping that should do it." He looked at the Figatellis. "There's a megaphone on the speedboat, right?" Florian nodded and gave him the thumbs up. "Good. Well, let's assume that the emergency medical team has talked its way on board. Here's where Daphne is crucial. Remember that I'm supposed to be a French doctor, and I only speak French. So, right at the start, Daphne will have to tell them that she will translate my instructions into English. If we need to, we can consult together in a corner, somewhere they can't hear my voice. All clear so far?"

Heads were nodding around the table. "OK. I'd like one policeman, Flo, to come aboard with Daphne and me. Jo stays in the speedboat in case anyone tries to slip away. Now here's the tricky part. We don't know what we're going to find on board. We don't know the boat's layout or where the hiding places might be. But I'm counting on the element of surprise. They won't be expecting us, and so Elena will probably be locked in one of the cabins." He stopped and looked around the table.

"If that's the case, it's possible they might refuse to unlock the door. That's when Flo gets nasty. Through Daphne, he'll tell them that they're obstructing official business, and if they don't open the door he'll kick it down. These are Englishmen we're dealing with, and they're not going to argue with a foreign police officer."

Philippe raised a hand. "Let's say everything goes according to plan," he said, "and you find Elena. How are you going to get her off the boat? Wapping and all the crew aren't going to just stand there and wave goodbye."

Sam nodded. "We talked about this coming over from

Corsica. The moment we find Elena, Flo will take out that ugly big gun of his and fire a shot—into the air, into the ceiling, through a porthole, it doesn't matter. A gunshot at close quarters does two things to people: it makes them scared and it makes them freeze. In this case, it will also be the signal for Jo to come up and join us. We will then have two armed men. I don't think anyone would be stupid enough to try his luck with two guns pointed at him. Also, Daphne and I have half a dozen syringes filled with a powerful anesthetic—one jab would make an elephant go down. And, as I said, we'll have surprise on our side. So we should be OK. Anything else?"

Flo raised a hand. "We need six glasses." He reached down and produced a dark-green bottle with a handwritten label. "We must drink to our success."

Sam laughed, and the tension left the room. "Why not?"

While Mimi was getting the glasses, Daphne asked Jo what was in the bottle. "*Myrte, chère madame, myrte*, the Corsican liqueur. Very good. I made it myself. We have a custom in the Figatelli family to drink a toast before we go out on a job. We have found it brings luck."

The glasses were filled, the mission was toasted, and Daphne, who was drinking *myrte* for the first time, gave a little shudder of pleasure as her first sip went down. "Oh my, that's very good indeed. Do you know, it reminds me of Owbridges." Seeing the blank looks around the table, she added, "It's a cough syrup I used to have as a girl at school. Delicious, and quite addictive—how we girls used to long to get a cough." She emptied her glass, looked down at the watch pinned to her bosom, and stood up. Sam could hear the dry whisper of starch against starch. "That did me a power of good," said Daphne. "Now I'm ready for anything."

Sam looked back at the house as they walked to the car. Philippe and Mimi, framed by the lighted doorway, were waving them off, and Philippe put his fist, thumb, and little finger extended, to his ear. "Call us as soon as you've got her."

Tension returned as the car made the short trip down to the Vieux Port. Sam took the syringes out of his bag and passed three to Daphne. "These work very quickly, and you don't need to find a vein. Neck, arm, wrist, anywhere there's a patch of bare skin." Daphne nodded, and arranged the syringes carefully in her empty breast pocket. "Mustn't get them confused with the thermometers, must we?" she said.

The cafés opposite the Vieux Port were still busy with after-dinner customers who were sitting outside, taking advantage of the gentle night air. The quay on the other side of the road was almost deserted, quiet enough to hear the creak of rigging as the boats rode the swell in their moorings. The Figatellis were leading the way, and they had almost reached the speedboat before Sam noticed a car parked on its own at the end of the quay. The headlights flashed once, then again. The others stopped to watch as Sam went over.

The back window slid down, and Sam was able to make out the familiar face of Francis Reboul. "I shall wait here until you come back," he said. He reached out of the window and grasped Sam's hand. "Good luck, my friend. Good luck."

# Eighteen

"Not too fast, Jo. We'd like to get there dry." Sam wiped the spray from his face and looked at his watch. He looked across at Daphne. She was in profile, and with her head held back and her redoubtable bosom, she made Sam think of a clipper ship's figurehead. She turned toward him and smiled. "What an adventure," she said, and then her face became serious. "I've been thinking, dear. Suppose someone asks us the name of this disease that we're looking for. What would we say?"

"Thank God you reminded me. I'm sorry—I should have told you earlier. The technical name is tropical spastic paraparesis. I came across it a few years ago when I was in Africa. We used to call it the Congo flux, and it's really nasty: drowsiness, fever, convulsions, vomiting, and death."

"Splendid," said Daphne.

"The curious thing about it is that it's spread by breath. If someone who is infected breathes on clothes or a handkerchief or a pillow, the virus stays contagious for several hours. In its early stages it's invisible. You don't know you've got it until the first symptoms appear."

"Is there a cure?"

"Induced total bodily evacuation, but that only works if you catch it within forty-eight hours."

Daphne nodded. "That should give them something to think about, if they ask. Oh, look! Isn't that *pretty*."

They had passed the tip of the island of Ratonneau and turned back into the Baie du Grand Soufre. There, at the end of the bay, *The Floating Pound* lay at anchor, lights blazing, a floating symbol of the capitalist dream come true. The Figatellis murmured their appreciation. "See that?" said Jo to his brother. "The helicopter parked on the stern? That is some piece of equipment. *Très sérieux.*"

Sam leaned forward. "Now, Jo. Once we're on board, I'd like you to park somewhere you can keep an eye on the helicopter. If anyone wants to make a quick getaway, that's what they'll try to use." Jo nodded, cut the engine until the boat was just making way, and glided closer to the yacht. They could see a crew member, in silhouette against the light flooding out from the main stateroom, take a final drag on his cigarette before flicking the butt over the rail and going back inside.

The speedboat eased gently up to the main gangway and came to a halt, riding easily on the swell. "OK," said Sam. "Here we go. Give them a shout."

Flo took the megaphone and requested permission to come aboard. They waited. No response.

"They don't understand French, obviously," said Daphne. "Here—let me have that." She took the megaphone and stood up, bracing herself against the speedboat's movement.

"Ahoy! *The Floating Pound!* Ahoy!" Her voice, a powerful instrument, bounced off the sea and echoed against the side of the yacht. "Medical emergency! I repeat, medical emergency!"

A figure appeared from a door behind the main stateroom and peered down at the speedboat.

"You there! Young man! I say again: this is a medical emergency. Now lower the gangway so the doctor can come aboard. Look sharp!"

A second figure appeared, and after a brief consultation the steps were lowered. A surprisingly nimble Daphne, followed by Sam and Flo, led the way on to the deck. She looked the two young crew members up and down, and clearly found them lacking in stature. "I need to speak to someone in authority at once," she said. They looked back at her, bleary-eyed and uncertain. *"At once!"*

The first test of Sam's disguise was about to take place. He adjusted his face mask and glasses and reminded himself that he didn't understand English, while a gnomelike figure, squinting in the half-light, came across the deck toward him.

"What's all this?" Ray Prendergast was not pleased. To obtain some relief from the increasingly tense atmosphere on the boat, he had settled down to watch an old favorite, the vintage DVD in which John Wayne single-handedly conquers Iwo Jima. And now this. He thrust his head toward Sam. "Who the hell are you? And what are you doing here?"

Sam looked at Daphne and shrugged, the picture of incomprehension. She took a step toward Prendergast and looked down at him from her superior height. "This gentleman is Dr. Ginoux. He unfortunately doesn't speak a word of English, but I can interpret for him. And I'm afraid we have some most disturbing and unpleasant news." She turned to Sam and, in rapid French, repeated what she had just said. Sam nodded, and waved a hand for her to continue.

"There is a strong possibility that two of the deckhands on a boat that arrived here recently from the Ivory Coast are infected by tropical spastic paraparesis. This is a viral disease that culminates in a slow and painful death unless it is discovered and treated in its early stages. It is also *extremely* contagious." Daphne paused to assess the effect her words were having on Prendergast, and was encouraged to see that his belligerent expression had been replaced by a frown.

She continued. "The quarantine authorities here in the port are treating this as an emergency, and have instructed us and several other medical teams to inspect all vessels that have recently arrived from ports outside France."

Prendergast's belligerent expression returned. "Wait a minute. This boat has come from England. We haven't been anywhere near the bloody Ivory Coast."

"I'm sorry, but the authorities are quite clear about this. It's possible, for instance, that some of your crew members may have had some contact with crew members from the infected vessel. Could you guarantee that no fraternization has taken place?"

Prendergast was silent.

"Of course you couldn't," said Daphne, "which is why, I'm afraid, we must inspect every cabin for traces of contagion. Fortunately, this can be done quite quickly by Dr. Ginoux. Now, if we could start with the master's cabin and work our way back, I think that would cause the least possible disruption."

Prendergast stopped chewing his lip. "I'll have to talk to the owner." He ducked back into the stateroom, leaving them on deck.

Daphne caught Sam's eye, and gave him a wink. "So far, so good, dear," she whispered. Flo, who had been quietly pacing the deck, came over to ask if he should go with them as they went through the cabins.

"Yes, definitely," said Sam. "When we find Elena, we're going to need you and your gun."

Five minutes turned into ten before Prendergast came back, this time with Lord Wapping, his bulk draped in a maroon silk dressing gown, brandy snifter in hand. He glanced briefly at Sam and Flo before turning his attention to Daphne. "You're the one who speaks English, right?" Daphne inclined her head. "Well then," said Wapping, "let's be sensible about this. I'm sure we don't have to get everybody out of bed at this time of night. I'm quite happy to sign something that says you've carried out the inspection, and then we can all get our kip." He took a sip of his brandy, looking at Daphne over the rim of his glass.

"I'm terribly sorry, but that won't be possible. Our instructions are . . ."

"Yes, yes, I know all about the instructions. Ray here told

me. But you know how the world works: a favor here, a favor there—I'm a generous man, know what I mean?"

Daphne turned to Sam and unleashed a torrent of French. When she'd finished, Sam said nothing. His index finger, wagging violently back and forth, and the emphatic shaking of his head was reply enough.

Daphne's voice was cold. "If there are any further attempts to obstruct this inspection, they will be reported to the appropriate authorities. And now, if you don't mind, we'll start with your cabin."

"Bloody waste of time." Wapping stalked back into the stateroom, followed by the others. Sam reached in his bag and put the light meter in his pocket.

Opening the door to Wapping's large and ornate cabin, they were greeted by the sight of Annabel sitting at her dressing table, brushing her hair. She was wearing a negligée of peach-colored silk, and at the sight of young Flo in his uniform she allowed one of the straps to slip a couple of inches down her suntanned shoulder. "What's happening?" she said, batting her eyelashes. "I do hope I'm not going to be arrested."

She seemed disappointed to be told that no arrest was imminent, and the team moved over to the double bed while Daphne explained the form the inspection would take. It was very simple. Dr. Ginoux would pass his detection device—a kind of Geiger counter for viral germs was how Daphne described it—over the pillows and the bathroom towels. If it indicated the signs of any infection, a reading would come up on the miniature screen; no signs of infection would be indicated by a different reading.

Watched by a glowering Lord Wapping and the pouting Annabel, Sam switched on his light meter and began to pass it across the surface of the pillows. The meter made impressive clicking noises, and tiny lights flashed on and off in a satisfying fashion each time the light density changed. Three minutes later, and the pillows were checked. Sam and Daphne moved into the bathroom, away from the view of spectators. *"C'est bon?"* They heard Daphne say, *"Pas de réaction négative? Très bien."*

She was smiling as they came back into the cabin. "There," she said brightly. "That didn't hurt a bit, did it? And now perhaps we can get on with the other cabins." Wapping stood in the cabin doorway nursing his brandy, watching them as they went down the main passageway toward the part of the boat where lesser mortals slept.

Their first stop was Ray Prendergast's cabin, where a low table showed traces of two of his passions. Recent copies of *The Racing Post*, the British horseracing bible, shared space with a comprehensive price list from Geoffrey's of Antibes (this week's special: Cottage Delight Tangy Orange English Breakfast Marmalade).

Prendergast, the picture of hostile suspicion, watched intently as Sam went through his routine, running the light meter up and down the bunk and across the pillows. When Sam moved into the tiny bathroom, Prendergast broke his silence. "You're not going to do this nonsense all through the boat, surely?"

"I'm afraid so," said Daphne, "all the cabins, of course. Then there's the kitchen, laundry room, storage room, even the engine room. Dr. Ginoux is extremely thorough, particularly with serious cases like this. Actually, it would be a great help if you could let us have a plan of the boat, just to make sure we don't miss anything."

Prendergast didn't reply. His mind was busy weighing the risks and possibilities, and as soon as the inspection team had left his cabin he started to make his way toward Lord Wapping's suite, only to meet his lordship coming down the passageway.

"Billy, we've got to do something."

"You're bloody right we have."

They went up to the sunbathing deck, where they could talk well away from any curious ears.

"She's down the far end, right? In the spare cabin."

Wapping nodded. "At the rate they're going, we've got about fifteen minutes to get her out of there. If they find her, the jig's up. Luckily, the boys gave her another jab this evening, so she won't be any bother. But where the hell can we put her? Get hold of Brian and Dave."

In Tiny de Salis's cabin, Daphne and Sam once again came across clues to the occupant's interests: the *Old Etonian Review*, published every Michaelmas, and a DVD entitled *Hot Babes—They Are Saucy and They Sizzle!* There was also an impressive stash of marijuana in an open cigar box on the bedside table. There was, however, no sign of de Salis himself.

Events in the passageway began to take on aspects of a French farce, with Brian and Dave ducking in and out of various doors until they came to the cabin being checked by Daphne and Sam. The door was ajar. Brian closed it gently and, using his passkey, locked it. They hurried down to the spare cabin.

It was a good five minutes before Brian came back and responded to the hammering on the cabin door. He was apologizing even as he unlocked it. "Sorry, miss," he said to Daphne, "it sometimes does this when the self-locking mechanism goes on the blink. Bloody nuisance, must get it fixed."

"What's the problem?" asked Ray Prendergast, solicitous for the first time, as he joined them in the passageway. Brian explained what had happened, Prendergast apologized again, asked if there was anything he could do, and insisted on staying with them while they checked the rest of the boat, "Just in case there's any more trouble with the doors."

They were just about to start on the next cabin when Daphne's phone rang.

"*Allo?*"

"It's Jo. Let me speak to Sam." Daphne saw that Prendergast was hovering, his eyes fixed on the phone. "*C'est l'hôpital,*" she said to Sam. "It's the hospital," she said to Prendergast. "I think it's best if Dr. Ginoux takes the call in private." She took Sam's arm, guided him into the cabin's shower room, and shut the door behind him.

"You know how they are about the phone, the French," she said to Prendergast. "Always want to be in their little private corner when they take a call."

Before speaking, Sam turned on the shower to make sure his voice didn't carry. "What is it, Jo?"

"Two men have been on deck here, right above me. I couldn't see them, but I could hear their voices. I think they were loading something into the helicopter."

Ray Prendergast would remember the next few seconds for a long time. The French doctor burst out of the shower room and started speaking fluent English to the police officer who was standing by the door. "Flo, you stay here with him." He jerked his head at the startled Prendergast. "If he tries to use his phone, break his arm. And if he tries to leave the cabin, knock him out and tie him up, OK? Daphne, you stay here—you'll be safe with Flo. I think they're trying to get out with Elena."

Sam ducked out of the cabin and raced up the passageway, through the main stateroom, and out onto the deck. The helicopter was a white mass at the far end of the boat. Much to his relief, he saw that the rotor blades were immobile. Moving more cautiously now and staying in the shadows as much as he could, he came to within a few yards of the helicopter. There was no sign of anybody. Now he was close enough to touch the helicopter. He reached up to open the door.

"What do you think you're doing?"

Sam turned to see Tiny de Salis, who had come around from the other side of the helicopter. He came closer. "Are you deaf? What are you doing?" He stood in front of Sam, legs braced apart, a big man ready to throw a punch.

Sam was not by nature a violent man, and it was with a twinge of genuine regret that he kicked de Salis in the testicles and pitched his writhing body overboard. Without waiting to hear the splash, he pulled open the door of the helicopter. And there, breathing easily, was the unconscious Elena in one of the back seats. Taking off his face mask, he climbed into the cockpit, stroked her face, held her tight. "You're safe now, girl. We'll have you home before you wake up."

Sam heard footsteps on the deck, reached in his pocket for a syringe, then relaxed when he saw who it was. "She's here, Jo. And she seems fine."

Jo's grin was a flicker of white in the shadows. "*Formidable*, Sam. *Vraiment formidable*. Oh, in case you were worrying about him, I fished your big friend out of the water, but he won't be going anywhere—I handcuffed him to the boat's steering wheel. What do we do now?"

Sam took out his phone. "First, we tell Francis. Then we get the police out here." He paused as the thought struck him. "Are they likely to be a problem? I mean, you're not exactly official."

"Don't worry. The story is that we're on special assignment from Corsica. The cops here can check with the police chief in Calvi. He's my uncle."

Sam spoke for a few minutes with a vastly relieved Reboul, who volunteered to arrange for the Marseille police to come out to the boat at once. Leaving Jo to guard Elena, he went back to the cabin, where he found Prendergast perched on the side of the bunk, his head sunk in his shoulders, staring at the floor. There was a cut on his forehead and a smear of blood on his face.

The reactions to Sam's good news were immediate and

enthusiastic: a smacking kiss on each cheek from Daphne, and a crushing bear hug from Flo. Prendergast's head seemed to have slumped even lower.

"Did he try anything?"

Flo nodded. "Only once."

Relief had made Sam feel intensely alive, slightly light-headed, and well disposed toward the world. With one notable exception. "The police will be here any minute now, and their first stop should be Wapping. Tell me, Flo—what's the penalty in France for kidnapping?"

The big man rubbed his chin. "That depends. If the victim has been harmed in any way, it's twenty-five years. If no harm has been done, it's only twenty years."

"Only twenty years. What are the jails like here?"

Figatelli assumed his most innocent expression. "I've had no personal experience, of course. But I've heard they're not exactly comfortable."

"Good. OK, let's get going." He turned to look at Prendergast, who had been listening closely, his expression a mixture of disbelief and despair. "Is there anywhere we can lock him up?"

Flo shrugged. "Why bother? I'll put him in with Wapping, and then stand outside the door until the cops come." He bent down and, none too gently, pulled Prendergast to his feet. The procession set off, reaching the master cabin just in time to welcome the Marseille police, who had arrived in force on two speedboats.

To Sam's relief, Flo had decided to deal with the situation himself. He told the captain in charge that the kidnapper was in the stateroom; that the victim was in a drugged sleep in the helicopter, saved from abduction by Sam; and that he and his colleagues were ready to be helpful in any way they could.

That, of course, was not the end of it. There were depositions to be taken, questions to be answered, and the curious appearance of two Corsican police officers to be explained. By the time this was over, what Daphne described as "dawn's rosy fingers" were touching the eastern horizon, and they were at last free to go.

Sam would always remember that short trip back to Marseille. Elena, still sleeping, was curled up in his arms, the sky was a misty pink, and the air smelled as though it had just been cleaned. Relief gave way to a deep, deep happiness.

As they were driving back to the house, Sam called Philippe, who picked up on the first ring.

"Good morning, my friend. I hope I didn't wake you up?"

"We haven't slept. What happened?"

As Sam finished going through the events of the night, a thought occurred to him. "Philippe, how would you like an exclusive? You know, kidnapper caught red-handed by Marseille's finest, his attempts to escape by helicopter foiled, all that stuff. I can fill you in on the details."

There was a moment of silence, then a grunt of approval from Philippe. "Not a bad idea. We'll make a journalist out of you yet."

# Nineteen

Elena stirred and turned over. With her eyes still half-closed, she reached out a hand, and when Sam took it, her face softened into a smile. "Oh, Sam, dear sweet Sam, where have I been? What time is it?"

"You took a day off. I'll tell you about it later. And it's breakfast time. Do you feel like having anything?"

"A shower. Coffee. A croissant. More coffee."

Despite Elena's protests, Sam insisted on helping her as she got out of bed. She stretched, kissed him, and walked into the bathroom as though she'd been through nothing more dramatic than a good night's sleep.

Back in the kitchen, Sam found Mimi on the phone and Philippe pounding away on his laptop. "Listen to this, Sam," he said, translating off the screen. "Millionaire Kidnap Suspect Helps Police with Their Enquiries—Beautiful Victim Rescued from Helicopter." He looked up at Sam. "Pretty good headline, don't you think? Mimi's trying to get hold of the editor before he gets into the office. He's going to love it. So will the police. They can always use some good press." Philippe waved Sam away and resumed his pounding, humming with satisfaction as he wrote. He barely noticed Mimi put down her phone and give him the thumbs up. "He likes it," she said, "but it's going to have to go through the lawyers. So if you could get it to him by lunchtime, that would be great."

Sam prepared a tray with coffee and croissants and went back into the bedroom, where Elena, in her terrycloth robe, was sitting on the edge of the bed. She inhaled the steam coming from her *café au lait*, dipped the end of her croissant in it, took a first bite, and grinned. "Now, Mr. Levitt. Tell me what happened. Did I have fun?"

The following morning saw Philippe's article on the front page of *La Provence*, illustrated by a photograph of Wapping's boat, with the helicopter on the stern clearly visible. Philippe had gone as far as the lawyers would allow, and anyone reading the piece would be left with the impression that *The Floating Pound* was manned by unsavory and possibly criminal foreigners. Those with a personal interest in the story were not slow in picking this up.

It completely ruined Jérôme Patrimonio's breakfast. This he liked to take in a café on the Vieux Port, where he was cultivating a clandestine relationship with the young wife of the elderly *patron*. But today there was no flirting, there were no lingering glances, no intimate moments as hands touched while the bill was being paid. The other regular customers were aware of Patrimonio's close connection with a veritable English lord—indeed, he frequently boasted about it—and one of them had shown him the article. He read it initially with a sense of shock, and then with increasing concern; not for Wapping, of course, but for himself. What would come out of the police investigation? Would he be implicated in any way? How could he protect himself as much as possible from any unpleasant repercussions? He left to go to his office, a distracted and worried man.

For Lord Wapping, too, the day started badly. He was under house arrest on the boat, his phone confiscated, his helicopter immobilized, police uniforms wherever he looked. He was enough of a realist to accept that he had been caught *en flagrant délit,* as one of the police officers had informed him (or, as Ray Prendergast put it, with his trousers round his ankles). This was bad enough, but it was not the only cloud on his horizon. Ever since the arrival of the police, Annabel had been behaving as if she hardly knew him.

Poor Annabel. She didn't need to see Philippe's article to know that she, and everyone else on the boat, would probably be treated as an accomplice to a criminal act unless she could prove that she had no knowledge of the kidnapping. In fact, this was almost the case. During her time with Wapping, she had developed a very efficient blind eye to what she called his business interests, and she had instinctively avoided asking any questions about the sleeping figure that Brian and Dave had brought on board. Now her mind was racing. If only she could find a way to get off the boat and over to her dear friends in Saint-Tropez. They would know what to do. It was all too, too ghastly.

For Patrimonio, the morning was rapidly spinning out of control. One after another, the members of the committee had called him to express their grave concerns about a known criminal being involved in a municipal project of this importance. There had also been a highly uncomfortable conversation with the mayor, who had told him in the most forceful language to take urgent steps to distance himself and his colleagues from Lord Wapping. With those angry words still fresh in his mind, Patrimonio had, as the mayor instructed, called an emergency meeting of the committee.

Not surprisingly, Francis Reboul's reaction to the story had been one of considerable satisfaction, mixed with a tinge of frustration. It seemed possible, even likely, that Wapping's bid would be disqualified, but Reboul's hands were tied. Officially, there was nothing he could do to encourage that decision. He needed to talk to Sam.

"How is Elena?"

"Francis, they make girls tough in California. It's as if nothing happened. She says she's feeling a little spacey, but otherwise fine. She's had breakfast, she's had a swim, and she's already talking about lunch and a glass of wine."

"I'm so pleased. And Sam—congratulations. You did a marvelous job. We must celebrate. But first, we need to tie up the loose ends and get the project approved, and as you know I can't do anything publicly to help."

Sam was already ahead of Reboul. "You know what I'd do if I were you? I'd get your friend Gaston to talk to his friend the mayor. He's Patrimonio's boss, so he must know what's going on."

And so it was agreed. When Reboul called Sam back, it was to tell him that, after talking to Gaston, the mayor had decided to attend the emergency meeting of the committee that was scheduled for the afternoon. Gaston had thought it useful to invite the mayor to dinner that same evening at Le Petit Nice. And, since no Frenchman in his right mind declines the offer of a three-star meal, the mayor canceled a previous engagement with the Marseille chapter of the Old Rotarians. Gaston was confident that, over what would undoubtedly be a magnificent dinner, the conversation would take a turn in the right direction.

The day was passing slowly for Lord Wapping and Ray Prendergast. Requests to have their cell phones returned had been refused, despite Wapping's plea that he needed to call his imaginary sick mother who was languishing in a London nursing home. They sat in the stateroom, their gloom only partly lifted by doses of brandy.

"Bastards," said Wapping. "They've got to let us call a lawyer, haven't they?"

"I don't know, Billy. The trouble is, they're French."

"Yes, Ray. I had noticed."

"What I mean is the rules and regs are different over here. Give you an example. They were still topping people—cutting their heads off—until 1981."

Wapping shuddered. "Bastards."

"That's not all. They don't like kidnappers, either. We're looking at twenty to twenty-five years in the slammer."

The two men sat in morose silence for several minutes. Wapping drained his glass and was reaching for the bottle when he stopped, his hand still in midair. "We need to get off the boat, right?"

Prendergast nodded.

"You've got to get me to a hospital."

"What's the matter?"

"Heart problems, Ray. Severe heart problems."

"I didn't know you had a dicky heart."

"I will have. Leave it to me."

The police officer on duty outside the stateroom glanced through the window just in time to see Lord Wapping topple from his chair and lie on the floor clutching his chest, his mouth gaping.

Jérôme Patrimonio called the meeting to order, somewhat inhibited by the presence of the mayor, an impassive figure at the far end of the conference table. In what he would later think of as one of his most effective performances as chairman, Patrimonio began by deploring the shocking behavior of Lord Wapping. Here was a man, he said, who had deceived them all, and had proved himself to be totally unsuitable as a partner in this vitally important project. Fortunately, his true character had been revealed before any commitments had been made. Also, Patrimonio went on, two other excellent schemes had been submitted, and the committee had already had ample time and information to consider each of them. And so, in the interests of fairness, democracy, and complete transparency, always close to his heart, he now proposed to put the matter to a vote. A simple show of hands around the table, he suggested, should be sufficient.

He looked at the mayor, slightly less impassive now, who nodded his approval. The members of the committee adjusted their expressions—grave and responsible, as befitted important men about to make an important decision. They were reminded by Patrimonio that they had the right to abstain.

The first proposal to be put to the vote was the hotel complex put forward by Madame Dumas on behalf of Eiffel International. Patrimonio looked around the table. Two hands were raised.

It was the turn of the second proposal, presented by Monsieur Levitt on behalf of the Swiss/American consortium. One by one, five hands went up, much to Patrimonio's relief; his decisive chairman's vote was not going to be necessary. He could not be blamed if anything went wrong.

"Well, gentlemen, I think we can agree that the committee has sent a very clear message, and I congratulate them on their decision." And with that, he shot his cuffs and declared the meeting closed.

Back in his office, Patrimonio made two calls: the first to a surprised Sam, the second to a senior editor at *La Provence*. Patrimonio's day, after a dreadful start, was beginning to look more promising.

# Twenty

"*Mais c'est pas possible*. I don't believe it." Philippe was laughing and shaking his head as he passed the morning's edition of *La Provence* across the breakfast table to Mimi. "Take a look. That rascal Sam—he never said a word to me about this."

Mimi put down her croissant, licked the flakes of pastry from her fingers, and spread the newspaper in front of her. There, above the fold on the front page, was a photograph of Patrimonio and Sam shaking hands and beaming into the camera. "A New Look for the Anse des Pêcheurs" read the headline, followed by several paragraphs of breathless prose that congratulated the committee on its difficult decision and emphasized the amicable and constructive relationship between Monsieur Jérôme Patrimonio and Monsieur Sam Levitt. The piece went on to announce that there would be a press conference shortly, when full details of the winning project would be revealed. The final seal of approval was provided by Patrimonio. "I am particularly pleased with the committee's decision," he said, "because this project was a personal favorite of mine from the very beginning."

On reading this, Mimi snorted, almost choking on her coffee. "*Qu'il est bestiasse!* What an idiot."

Philippe was still grinning. "Now there's a press conference I'd hate to miss. Want to come?"

Following the arrest of Lord Wapping and his crew, Philippe and Mimi had decided that it was safe to move back into his apartment. As a result, they had been seeing less of Sam. "Leave him alone for a minute," said Philippe, "and he starts mixing with all kinds of weird people." He reached for his phone and tapped in Sam's number.

"Is that Monsieur Sam Levitt, who has an amicable and constructive relationship with that horse's ass Patrimonio?"

Sam groaned. "I know, Philippe, I know. Don't be too hard on me. He called and said it was important that we meet at his office. When I got there, he'd just finished an interview with one of your guys on the paper. Then the photographer comes in . . ."

"And the rest is history. I bet he was wearing makeup for the shot. Now tell me—when's the press conference?"

"Tomorrow afternoon. His secretary's calling around to the media this morning. You can come, but only if you behave yourself."

"*Moi?* Misbehave? I shall be a perfect example of the professional journalist."

"That's what I'm afraid of. See you tomorrow."

"Now, my dear Monsieur Levitt, it would probably be best if I handled all the questions," Patrimonio said, glancing around the conference room, searching the walls in vain for a mirror. He was at his sartorial best for the occasion, in a cream silk suit, pale-blue shirt, and his treasured Old Etonian tie. "Of course, if I need to consult you on a technical matter, I will. But I think it best if there is one official spokesman for the project, don't you agree?"

"Absolutely," said Sam, who was more than happy to let Patrimonio take the questions. He was already enjoying the delightful irony of the situation: Here was Patrimonio promoting the project of his old enemy Reboul. "Apart from anything else," Sam said, "your French is so much better than mine."

Patrimonio's secretary put her head around the conference room door. "I think they're all here," she said.

"Show them in, my dear. Show them in." Patrimonio went through his ritual of hair-smoothing, cuff-shooting, and tie-tweaking before assuming a welcoming smile as the media filed in. A three-man television crew from a local station was followed by half a dozen writers from the specialist press—design and architecture, *Côté Sud* magazine—and a small troop of real-estate agents anxious to get a foot in the door. Bringing up the rear was Philippe. At the sight of him, Patrimonio's smile faltered for a second before he recovered.

In his presentation, Patrimonio was careful to allocate

credit where it was due; that is, to himself. There he was, the steady hand of guidance at every stage of the process, from choosing the short list to overseeing the final decision. It was, if you believed what you heard, the story of one man's dedication and sound judgment. Halfway through, Sam made the mistake of catching Philippe's eye, and was rewarded by an exaggerated wink.

When Patrimonio finally stopped, the questions, as he had hoped, were soft. How much would the project cost? What was the schedule of work, and when would it start? What were the purchase arrangements for the finished apartments? Patrimonio gave adequately optimistic answers, and was congratulating himself on the smooth progress of the meeting when Philippe cleared his throat loudly and raised his hand.

"Monsieur Patrimonio," he asked, "what has happened to the millionaire kidnapper? I understand he was on the short list. You two were quite friendly, weren't you? Any news about him?"

But Patrimonio, a man well versed in the art of evasion, had no intention of going anywhere near that particular subject. "For legal reasons, I can't possibly comment on that. It's a matter for the police." He consulted his watch. "And now, ladies and gentlemen, unless there are any further questions, Monsieur Levitt and I have work to do."


Reboul had decided that the decision called for a celebration. It was still too soon, he felt, to be seen publicly in Marseille with Sam and Elena, and so he had made arrangements for what he called "a little country lunch." Two cars would come to the house to take Elena, Sam, Mimi, Philippe, and Daphne to a discreet restaurant hidden away in the Luberon. Reboul would meet them there.

At eleven o'clock sharp, two black Mercedes pulled into the driveway of the house. The two young chauffeurs, in black suits and sunglasses, guided the passengers to their seats, and they set off. Daphne had asked to travel with Elena and Mimi—"all girls together, dear, so we can gossip about you two," as she said to Sam—leaving the men to follow in the second car.

In little over an hour they found themselves in a completely different world. After the crowds and concrete and sea views of Marseille, the Luberon looked lush and deserted. The rains of spring had helped to give the mountains a covering of every shade of green, fresh and shining, and the sky was postcard blue. It was perfect weather for lunch, as Philippe said to Sam.

The final part of the drive took them up the narrow, twisting road that climbs to the top of the Luberon until they came to a painted wooden sign, half-obscured by ivy, that announced Le Mas des Oliviers. An arrow pointed down a stony track that wound through fields of olive trees, silver-green leaves shivering in the breeze, and ended at the high walls and open gates of the restaurant. Framed in the opening, a broad smile on his face, stood Reboul.

He was introduced to Daphne, Mimi, and Philippe, kissed Elena and Sam, and led them into a vast courtyard, easily large enough for the two mature chestnut trees whose leaves provided shade for a long table. Sam noticed that it was laid for eight. "Don't tell me you invited Patrimonio?"

Reboul grinned. "Certainly not. But Sam, I have a new friend—ah, there she is." Sam followed Reboul as he went over to the doorway of the main restaurant. "My dear, this is Sam, who has been such a help to me. Sam, I'd like you to meet Monica Chung." She was tiny, barely up to Sam's shoulder, with glossy black hair and almond eyes, no longer young but still beautiful, and extremely elegant. Even Sam, no expert, could tell that her silk dress had come from Paris. He bowed over her hand, and Reboul nodded his approval. "You know, you're beginning to act like a civilized Frenchman."

As they crossed the courtyard to join the others, Reboul slipped his arm round Monica's waist. "Monica and I have mutual interests in Hong Kong. She's a ferocious business-woman, and an excellent cook, but I must warn you, Sam, never play mah-jongg with her—she'll murder you." Monica laughed. "We've had two thousand years of training, Francis. Now, who are these nice people?"

While the introductions were being made, a couple came out to join them carrying trays with bottles and glasses and ice. "This is Mireille," said Reboul, "who does wonderful things in the kitchen. And this is her husband, Bernard, who insists that we have an apéritif before we eat." They were a cheerful couple, living testimonials to Mireille's cooking, plump and jovial. They distributed pastis and glasses of *rosé* before Mireille made her excuses and disappeared to supervise the preparations for lunch while Bernard fussed over the table settings.

The courtyard was an art director's dream. The drystone walls, two feet thick and ten feet high, had turned a soft gray over several hundred years of weather, their color matched by the pockmarked flagstones of the floor. Massive Anduze pots of faded terra-cotta, planted with scarlet geraniums and white lobelia, lined the walls, and a selection of straw hats—in case any sun should penetrate the leaves—had been hung on the trunks of the chestnut trees.

The lunch lived up to the surroundings. It was a parade of Mireille's favorite dishes, starting with an appetizer of *beignets de fleurs*, flash-fried zucchini flowers. These were followed by tarts of anchovies and olives on a bed of softened onions—the classic *pissaladière* of Nice. The main dish, Mireille's favorite of favorites, was a *charlotte* of lamb and aubergines, served with potatoes roasted in goose fat. Then a little cheese, provided by an obliging local goat. And finally, a soup of peaches topped with sprigs of fresh verbena. A lunch, so Bernard told them, that would set a man up for a hard afternoon's work in the fields.

Wine and conversation flowed, and nearly three hours passed before Reboul rose to his feet and tapped his glass with a spoon for attention.

"My friends," he said, "this is a very happy day, and I don't want to spoil it with a long speech. But I can't let the occasion pass without offering my admiration and thanks to Sam, and I hope he will accept this token of my appreciation." He walked round the table to where Sam was sitting, and presented him with an envelope.

Sam opened it. Inside was a check for one million dollars. He blinked, then looked up at Reboul. Both men were smiling, but it was a few moments before Sam could speak.

"Lunch is on me," he said.

### CHASING CÉZANNE

Camilla Jameson Porter, editor of the glossy magazine *Decorating Quarterly*, has commissioned Andre Kelly to photograph the treasures of the rich, famous, and fatuous. After Andre spots a priceless Cézanne being loaded onto a plumber's truck near a collector's home, he begins a riotous quest through galleries, glamorous houses, and enticingly delectable restaurants.

Fiction

### HOTEL PASTIS

Simon Shaw, a rumpled, fortyish English advertising executive has decided to chuck it all and transform an abandoned police station in the Lubéron into the small but world-class Hotel Pastis. On his side, he has a loyal majordomo and a French business partner who is both practical and ravishing. But he hasn't counted on the malignant local journalist—or on the *mauvaise* types who have chosen the neighboring village as the site of their latest bank robbery.

Fiction

### THE VINTAGE CAPER

The story begins high above Los Angeles at the impressive wine cellar of lawyer Danny Roth. Unfortunately, after inviting the *Los Angeles Times* to write an extensive profile extolling the liquid treasures of his collection, Roth finds himself the victim of a world-class wine heist. Enter Sam Levitt, former lawyer and wine connoisseur, who follows leads to Bordeaux and Provence.

Fiction

### A YEAR IN PROVENCE

In this witty and warmhearted account, Peter Mayle realizes a long-cherished dream and moves into a two-hundred-year-old farmhouse in the remote French countryside. *A Year in Provence* transports us into all the earthy pleasures of Provençal life and lets us live vicariously at a tempo governed by seasons, not by days.

Travel

## TOUJOURS PROVENCE

Taking up where *A Year in Provence* left off, Peter Mayle offers another funny and deliciously evocative book about life in the South of France. With tales of finding gold coins while digging in the garden and indulging in sumptuous dinners at truck stops, *Toujours Provence* is a charming portrait of a place where, if you can't quite "get away from it all," you can surely have a good time trying.

Travel

## ENCORE PROVENCE

After attempting—what folly!—to live in other places, Peter Mayle is back in his beloved Provence. He celebrates his homecoming by sharing with us a whole new feast of adventures, discoveries, mishaps, and culinary treats, liberally seasoned with a joyous mix of Gallic characters. Here, too, are Mayle's tips on where to find the best cheese and *chambre d'hôte* the region has to offer.

Travel

## FRENCH LESSONS

*French Lessons* is an ebullient exploration of the infinite gastronomic pleasures of France. Armed with knife, fork, and corkscrew, Peter Mayle travels to every corner of the country to visit tiny, out-of-the-way restaurants, starred Michelin wonders, annual festivals, local village markets, and blessed vineyards.

Travel

### ALSO AVAILABLE
*Anything Considered*
*A Good Year*
*A Dog's Life*
*Provence A–Z*

VINTAGE BOOKS
Available wherever books are sold.
www.vintagebooks.com